PAUL VANDORN

Challenging Entropy

To my readers who have been with me from the beginning, this one's for you. I truly appreciate your support.

A special thank you to my dear friends, Tammy Kleveno and Mike Ashe.

I think you should always bear
in mind that entropy is not on
your side.

~ Elon Musk

Prologue

CHALLENGING ENTROPY

Friday, May 10, 2019
Tabor County, Iowa

The blisters on the backs of Joey Parks' heels barked with every squish of his size 6 sneakers. Making matters worse, Joey hadn't eaten or slept in the last 24 hours, and he felt sick to his stomach. The rain that had drenched his little search party through the night had finally let up, but water continued to drip from the leafy canopy above.

It had been the most miserable 24 hours of his life, and that was saying something when you were the younger brother of a monster like Billy Parks.

"Frickin' Billy," he muttered to himself and felt a shudder run through his body at the mere thought of his big brother.

Big brothers were supposed to look out for little brothers. They were supposed to protect them. But Billy wasn't like other big brothers. Billy Parks was Joey's living, breathing, walking nightmare. Instinctively, Joey looked back over his shoulder, fully expecting to see Billy sneaking up from behind. Getting clobbered and dragged off into the woods to be murdered by that psycho made perfect sense in his 12-year-old brain.

What he saw was his mother. Her auburn hair hung in bedraggled strands that framed a sad, tired smile. Even as a kid, Joanna Parks had always looked a little older than she was. Probably the reason she always attracted the older boys. Like the one that got her pregnant. But on this wet spring morning, Joanna looked twice her age. And knew Joey why. "Frickin' Billy," he said again. This time, a little louder.

"Joey Parks, Billy is your brother," Joanna said sternly.

"Sorry, Mom."

And he was sorry. Not for frickin'. The epithet fit. Joey was sorry that Billy was his brother. If it weren't for Billy, they wouldn't have been out slogging through the rain-drenched woods all night. His mother wouldn't be aging twice as fast as she should be, and he wouldn't have suffered such a miserable existence. Especially since his piece of shit father had gotten sent away.

But Billy's not here, he thought, *and if I'm lucky, I'll never see him again.* A smile bloomed on Joey's face. Billy might have finally gone too far. *Maybe the cops will find him... find him and shoot him in his stupid head.* Joey squeezed his lips together to keep the smile from growing any larger. But who was he kidding? Billy never got what he deserved, and besides, he was probably a hundred miles away by now. Joey's smile faded, but just a little.

Detective Kevin Sullivan grunted and dragged a wet, dirty hand across his face. "Are you sure it's out here?"

"I'm sure, sir," Joey said, trying his best to sound confident.

"Listen, Joey, if you're just stalling us so your brother has time to—" "I'm not! I swear."

"Detective, enough is enough," Joanna Parks chided. "I agreed to let Joey try to help you find your friend, and now you're accusing him of—" "I'm not accusing him of anything, Mrs. Parks. But we've been going in circles all night." Then, re-directing his attention and softening his tone, "Joey, are you sure it was a body and not just a pile of leaves or—" "No, sir! I'm positive," Joey shouted, and then, in a softer voice, "Maybe an animal dragged him off."

Sullivan shook his head. "Not likely, kid. We don't have any predators large enough to drag a full-grown man away, not around here."

"Son, are you sure you're being straight with us?" asked Deputy Jeff Anderson, who had volunteered to help with the search. "We've been at this all night, kid."

"Yes, sir," Joey said. He could feel the area around his nose and cheeks warming and was afraid that he might start bawling. "I swear."

"Detective Sullivan," Joanna barked and then softened. "It's been a long night." She placed her hands on her son's shoulders and pulled him to her. "Joey's done all he can. I'm sorry you can't find what you're looking for, but I'm taking him home now."

Joey pulled away from her. "No, Mom, I know I can find him. I just need to start from the tracks."

Sullivan stooped, his hands on his knees. "What tracks are you talking about, Joey?"

"The train tracks, down by the river," he said. "I know how to get there from the tracks." He looked sheepishly at his mother. "Mom, we only took the shortcut because we were gonna be late."

If she'd told them once, she had told them a thousand times not to take the shortcut through Dunn's Hollow. "Oh, my God." Joanna clamped her hand over her mouth. "This is my fault?"

"I didn't want to take it, Mom. I know you told us not to, but Billy said it would be okay."

"Am I missing something?" Sullivan asked.

"It's haunted," Joey said.

Joanna swiped her wet hair away from her face.

"It really is my fault."

"What do you mean, haunted?" Sullivan asked.

"There was a little boy named Richie." Joey hung his head. "He disappeared, and they found him there."

"Richie Barrett?"

"Yes, sir. None of us kids go through those woods anymore, even though it's a good shortcut. Not since Richie got..."

"I don't understand; what does Richie Barrett have to do with this?"

"The dead body is next to the bridge where they found Richie. I thought I could find my way back there, but-"

Detective Sullivan looked around as if he were getting his bearings. "I know where that is," he said and set off at a quick pace.

"Hey, wait. That means you don't need us anymore, right?" Joanna asked.

Sullivan halted. "Mrs. Parks, if you could please just bear with us a little longer. We're so close. We've just been on the wrong side of the creek. It's no wonder he couldn't find it in the dark."

Joanna exhaled and rolled her eyes. "I'll give you 20 more minutes, then I'm taking my son back home."

"We'll only need half that, Mrs. Parks." Sullivan took a hard right. "This way," he said.

"You guys never did catch that son of a bitch, did you?" Her tone harsh and accusatory.

"No, ma'am, we didn't."

"My dad said a crazy person got him, Richie, I mean," Joey added.

"I don't know, kid. All I know is that nobody reported Richie missing. His parents thought he'd spent the night at a friend's house. That was my second year on the job, and I almost quit. That fucking monster chopped that kid to pieces."

"Detective, please!" Joey's mom had clamped her hands over his ears, but it didn't matter; Joey heard every word.

"Sorry, ma'am."

"Why didn't you quit?" Joey asked.

"What?" Sullivan asked, still lost in the memory.

"You said you almost quit. Why didn't you?"

Sullivan jutted his chin. "It was Deputy Anderson. He told me that the world is full of monsters." A sad smile settled briefly on Sullivan's face. "He told me that the good guys can't quit, because it's our job to hunt the monsters."

"Cool," Joey said. The thought of being a monster hunter thrilled the boy. He imagined himself decked out in police tactical gear hunting Billy. The musing rose in his mind and then burst like a soap bubble as Billy's face shoved its way into his daydream.

"Hunting and catching are two different things," Joanna reminded coldly.

"No shit," Sullivan said.

They hurried on without speaking. The only sounds came from nature and the squish of the water bubbling out of their shoes. Finally, they arrived at the footbridge. "Hm, it's smaller than I remember," Sullivan said and started across. Joey, who trailed behind, could almost feel his feet growing heavier with each step.

Slick and moss-covered, the bridge looked like something out of a fairy tale. But not the watered-down pablum served to today's youth. This bridge could have been pulled from the original writings of the Brothers Grimm. The fairy tales that fueled the nightmares of German children in the 1800s.

No more than ten feet across with a gentle arch at the middle, the bridge was the only remaining man-made landmark around. Gone were the wooden crosses, teddy bears, and grandiose floral arrangements that once marked the site. Richie's family had moved away. The mourners and well-wishers stopped showing up, and in time, nature reclaimed all that was left behind. All but the bridge.

Detective Sullivan stepped off the far end, but when Joey reached the other side, he froze in his tracks.

"What's wrong, honey? And what's that buzzing

sound?" Joanna asked.

"Flies," Joey said and pointed toward a clearing beyond a small berm just ahead. "We're here."

"Detective?" Joanna called.

"Yeah?" He turned to see that she and Joey weren't following. "What's wrong?"

"Joey said that we're here." Joanna nodded toward a low hedgerow.

Sully walked through a thin line of brush and into a clearing just as the wind shifted. The smell was horrendous and hit Joey just as he was inhaling. He stifled the urge to barf. A task made easier because his stomach was empty, and pushed back against his mother. Joanna Parks wrapped an arm around her son and pressed the back of her free hand to her nose and mouth. "What is that smell?"

"Fuck!" Sullivan shook his head. "Hey Jeff, when did you say he went missing?"

"Yesterday at 17:30. Why?" Jeff Anderson replied as he stepped into the clearing and saw the body. "Holy shit, that can't be..."

"It is," Sully said, pointing to the nameplate on his shirt.

"I don't understand. It's only been..." Anderson looked down and started counting on his fingers.

"Neither do I," Sully said, as he scanned the area before locking in on his next discovery. "Anderson," he said, jutting a finger toward the south where another body lay not 30 feet away.

"Shit."

"Shit is right. I'm guessing that's our killer," Sullivan suggested and looked over at Joey. "Hey Joey! Was this other body here yesterday, son?"

Joey dropped his head and answered under his breath. "There's something I have to tell you."

"What?" Sullivan called out.

"Joey said he has something to tell you," Joanna responded, not taking her eyes off of her son.

1

Chapter 1

Thursday, May 9, 2019
Oehlerking Farm – Rural Iowa

Rodney Oehlerking shielded his eyes against the glare that streamed through the broken slats of his bedroom blinds and studied the dust motes that floated and danced on the shafts of sunlight that fell across his bed. He hadn't invited them into his house, but still, there they were, thousands of them, perhaps hundreds of thousands. Rodney passed a hand through the beam, scattering the tiny particles, and marveled at how quickly they fell back into place. No matter how many times he tried, he could not disrupt the dancers for more than a few seconds, and he felt a tinge of jealousy at their implacability.

It moved through the old lead pipes that wormed like intestines through the house, falling warm and then scalding hot from the calcium-encrusted shower head.

He could have opted to wait and let the water warm up before he got in, but that just wasn't his way. Rodney showered and stepped out onto the bathroom floor, sopping wet. The water dripped off his body, seeping through the cracks in yellowing linoleum and soaking into the rotting wood of the floor joists below. He paused to regard himself in front of the mirror. Despite the slight hunch in his back, Rodney was still over six feet tall. He had broad shoulders, an unnaturally long neck, and a remarkably large Adam's apple. His arms and legs, though spindly, were roped in muscle, and he admired the image reflected back at him. Naked as a jaybird, Rodney Oehlerking walked into the kitchen, where he opened the breadbox and removed two pieces of slightly moldy bread from the bag. He'd bought the loaf less than a week ago, but that didn't matter; nothing lasted at his place. Rodney struck a match, lit the pilot light on his stove, and set the coffee pot on the burner. Then he dropped the bread into the toaster and grabbed the margarine, which he called grease, out of the fridge. As always, the light didn't turn on when he opened the door. Rodney had given up on replacing the bulb about six years ago and had all but stopped noticing, but for some reason, the darkness bothered him this morning. Reaching into the fridge, he flicked a thick yellow fingernail at the bulb, causing it to flash a few times before going out again.

Rodney swore and slammed the door shut as the bread in the toaster began to smoke. Forcing the lever up, he unplugged the appliance and sighed. It wasn't that he had to eat burnt toast; he'd grown accustomed to the taste over the years. It was more just the state of things that had him out of sorts. Rodney grabbed a tarnished butter knife from the drawer, slathered the grease over the burned bread, and poured a cup of four-day-old coffee. He was already moving with less pain. Showers always seemed to help—which was good because there was much to do.

Rodney set his breakfast on the table and walked back into his bedroom. The wooden legs of his bed screeched across the wooden floor as he pushed it aside and dropped back down to his knees. The movement came easier than it had for morning prayers. He worked his thick fingernails between the tight-fitting slats and lifted one of the floor-boards. He lowered his hand carefully into the opening, which he had booby-trapped with razor wire and broken glass against any would-be bur-glars. From the hole in his floor, he removed a small wooden box. The box was light in his hands, making a slight rattle as he walked. The sound caused him to smile, exposing teeth that had never visited a dentist. He carried the treasure back to his table, where he sat bare-assed on a hard wooden chair, eating burnt toast and drinking stale coffee.

After breakfast, Rodney returned his box to its hiding place and dressed for the day. He pulled on his wool socks and green corduroy pants, stuck his head and arms through his moth-eaten dago-tee, yellowed by age and sweat, and finished that off with a thick red-and-blue flannel. Rodney jammed his feet into his worn work boots and topped his almost completely bald dome with a knit cap under which hung long, gray strands of hair that reached out like the tentacles of some ancient sea creature. Before leaving, he cleaned his cup and dish and returned them to their proper places. He was meticulous that way. Rodney threw on his heavy, brown canvas jacket, locked the door behind him, and double-checked it before stepping out into the cold mist that clung to the air. It was spring, but none of the trees around his place showed any signs of life. The fields his father had tended, once lush and full of life, now were wind-raked and barren. The small creek that ran through his backyard had dried up years ago. Neither Winter's thaws nor spring, with its heavy rains, could ever bring it back. Rodney climbed into his car, rested his head against his steering wheel, and began to cry. He loved his home and land, but like his body, they too had been blighted by some unseen wasting entity. Composing himself, Rodney turned the key in the ignition, a 50-50 proposition at best. To his surprise, the unremarkable blue sedan started.

He reached the end of his gravel driveway and turned left, driving along the dead hedgerow he had laid in by hand over the years to block the view from the road. It was probably unnecessary—no one ever traveled past his house, but he couldn't be too careful. The road leading to his property had no name. It didn't need one. He had no visitors, and not even the postman made it this far off the main road. The latter caused Rodney to drive into town to pick up his mail once a week, but that was fine with him. He preferred the solitude of the country to the overcrowding of towns and cities. Rodney dialed in the classical station out of Cedar Falls; even this far out, the signal came in strong, and it would only get stronger the closer he got to the city. As he drove, he began to cry again, not for his home or his land, but for what he must do. Rodney hated it but had to keep trying until he got it right.

2

Chapter 2

Friday, May 10, 2019
U.S. Marshals' Office – Omaha, Nebraska

The phone that sat atop the cluttered desk in the Nebraska District Office of the U.S. Marshal Service jumped in its cradle. National Jones could hear it ringing as he stepped off the elevator and dashed down the carpeted hall towards his office door. He fumbled for his key, trying not to spill his hot coffee, a task made all the more difficult by the key wallet in which he kept it. The wallet, an archaic device used to silence noisy jangling keys, had been a gift from his father. Jones hated the damned thing, but he could never get rid of it. His father, Everett, had made the sixteen-hour drive down from Davenport to F.L.E.T.C., the Federal Law Enforcement Training Center, in Glynco, Georgia, to see his son graduate.

"Here, son," his father said as he handed him the small, poorly wrapped box. "Don't let the bastards hear you coming."

He never knew who the bastards were that his father had alluded to, and he never got to ask him. Everett Jones had been killed in a head-on crash on his way home from the graduation ceremony. It happened in southern Illinois, just east of Scott Air Force Base. A drunk driver turned onto I-64 in the wrong direction at the Highway 4 interchange. The doctor said that he didn't suffer, but that was cold comfort to a young man who had just lost the last person in the world who had loved him unconditionally.

Jones's mother, Elizabeth, who everyone called Lizzie, had died of cervical cancer when he was only nine years old. Ten years later, she was joined in the afterlife by his sister Emma. While attending college in New York, Emma was beaten to death by a jealous boyfriend. The guy was never convicted. Hell, he wasn't even charged. And it should've been an open and shut case. She had told her friends that if anything happened to her, if she ever vanished, tell the police that Richard did it. Her friends said that he'd given her a couple of good beatings and told her that he knew how to get rid of a body. Some people in Jones's family said that it was because he was a white boy. Jones knew race had nothing to do with it. Emma's body was found on September 20, 2001, just nine days after the attack at the World Trade Center, and the N.Y.P.D. had bigger fish to fry. Nevertheless, his sister's murder was a key factor in his decision to pursue a career in law enforcement.

Jones balanced the cup on his wrist and pinched the lid between his teeth as he unzipped the wallet. Hot, moist air rose up out of the sipping hole and steamed his upper lip. Naturally, his bite slipped, and the cup hit the floor, blowing its lid and splashing hot coffee everywhere.

"Shit! Hang on, hang on, I'm coming."

He touched his upper lip with the tip of his tongue. He was sure there would be a blister. Jones sunk the key into the lock, twisted the knob, and dashed for his desk just as the phone stopped ringing.

"Jones here," he said, snatching the receiver from the cradle, but it was too late. He'd burned his lip, spilled coffee on his red snakeskin boots, and still managed to miss the call.

Maybe it was just as well. He was sure it was Deputy Director Crenshaw calling to chew him a new asshole. Jones had gotten himself involved, unofficially, in a local drug bust that went pear-shaped with the execution of the case's lead witness. Three days ago, on the day he was set to tes-tify, Mike "The Slob" Slobada, a low-level shitbag dealer, showed up on the courthouse lawn in three separate plastic garbage bags. In his defense, Jones had requested that Slobada be placed under the protection of the US Marshal's Service until the trial was over, but the deputy director denied the request as it was not a federal case. Jones knew Crenshaw was right, and he kicked himself for getting involved. He tossed his keys, hat and briefcase onto his desk and walked into the break room, where he grabbed a wad of paper towels. He dabbed at his boots, hoping the coffee wouldn't leave a stain.

"Son-of-a... I paid $300 for these."

He tossed the wad in the trash, balled up another bunch of paper towels and started for the hallway, where the bigger mess lay. On his way, he grabbed a trash can and set it in the doorway to hold it open. As he squatted down on the floor, making a third and final pass over the spill, his phone rang again. Jones popped up and knocked over the trash can. As the door started to close, he glanced toward his desk and caught the glint of his keys sitting in the middle of the green blotter. Jones shoved his hand forward into the gap just in time to catch his fingertips between the door and the door jamb. The pain bit deep into his nail beds, and he cursed loudly all the way to the phone.

"Jones here," he barked.

"Nation, where the hell have you been? I've been trying to get ahold of you for the last two hours."

Jones didn't have to ask who was calling; he recognized the voice immediately. He pulled his cellphone from his pocket and looked at the screen. It showed that he'd missed eight calls from his childhood friend.

"Sorry, I had my phone on silent and didn't feel the buzz. How you been, Sabo?"

"Not good. Look, I need your help. We have a missing girl, and I..."

"A missing girl? Dude, you know we don't handle missings unless they're fugitives.

"I know, but..."

"Call the F.B.I. if the locals can't handle it."

"Those uptight assholes? They don't give a shit. I know you, Nation; you're obsessive, and that's what I need right now. You're what I need, brother," he paused. She's a good kid, Nation."

Jones rolled his eyes. "She a friend of yours?" he asked suspiciously.

"No, man, she's just—"

"Look, Sabo," Jones interrupted, "I'd love to help you out, but I'm up to my eyeballs in my own shit down here. I fucked something up, and my boss is pissed. I can't afford to be—"

"Nation, you better sit down." There was a slight tremble in Sabo's voice.

Jones had never known Sebastian Serradella to sound worried. Sabo had been a lead homicide investigator and a rising star in their hometown of Davenport, Iowa. He'd been involved in several officer-involved shootings, worked more major cases and closed them with arrests than any cop he'd ever known. But as good as he was, his cavalier attitude and his fondness for booze and women derailed what was a promising career, and through it all, he had never known Sabo to sound worried.

About seven years back, Sabo wrapped his car around a tree with the mayor's wife in the passenger seat. What she was doing in his car and why he crashed was never made public record, but the mayor made it his life's work to ruin Sabo. He lost his job and his pension, and no department in the state would hire him. Sabo's response? Shit happens. Blackballed, he had to take work where he could find it, and the last Jones heard, he was working as a security guard on a college campus. Jones imagined him spending his time chasing co-eds and drinking with the frat boys. Sabo was a guy who never took anything seriously. So if he sounded worried, Jones would be willing to bet the farm that whatever it was, it was worth worrying about.

"Okay, I'm sitting down."

"Listen, man, this missing, she ain't no ordinary missing."

"What, she got rich parents?"

"No, man, nothing like that. Just listen. We got Charlotte Rittenhouse from Major Crimes out here."

"That name supposed to mean something to me?"

"Back before I got shit-canned, I worked with her on a task force. She's one of the best detectives I've ever seen."

"Yeah? So, if you got Major Crimes and Super Detective on this, what do you need with me?"

"Nation," Sabo paused, and Jones could hear his throat click as he swallowed. "They're working two other cases involving missing girls in the area."

The hairs on Jones's neck stood up.

"Charlotte said that they found one of the girls in the Shell Rock River. The girl was missing part of her two front teeth."

Sabo's voice seemed to trail off, like he was talking to him through two soup cans attached by twine. Jones didn't respond.

"Nation, did you hear me? The killer snapped out her teeth."

The receiver almost fell from his hand. Like Sabo, National Jones had suffered his own fall from grace. As a rookie, Jones racked up an impressive 22 apprehensions in his first three years of service. There was some talk that the higher-ups might be looking to groom him to head a district office someday. About five years into his career, Jones was asked to consult on a series of murders in Chicago. He'd been working out of the Northern Illinois District Office on Dearborn Street when a detective he'd met early on in his career called him for assistance with an investigation involving a series of murders, strictly off the books.

In all, six bodies were recovered, one each from the lagoons at McKinley Park, Douglas Park, Marquette Park, Humboldt Park, and Jackson Park, right beneath the Nancy Hays Bridge. The final body, the one that hit him the hardest, was pulled from the Lake of Memories in Chicago's Oak Wood Cemetery. In each case, the girl had been bled dry, dressed in a crudely sewn white linen dress, and each was missing the bottom halves of their upper central incisors. According to the medical examiners in each case, the cause of death was a combination of strangulation, not surprising given the deep ligature marks on their necks, and bleeding out by way of severing their dorsal pedis arteries.

As for the missing teeth, they weren't the result of some congenital abnormality or accidents. They had been clipped or snapped off antemortem. The newspapers had dubbed it "The Tooth Fairy Killings," and during the summer of 2010, it was all anyone was talking about in Chicagoland. By the time the fourth body was discovered, the story had gone national. And then came the now infamous quote from US Marshal National Jones.

During a momentary lapse in judgment, one that it seemed would dog him for the rest of his career, Jones said, "We are going to get the Tooth Fairy, I guaran-fucking-tee it." In his defense, the newspaper reporter from the Town Journal had accosted him as he walked up the hill from the Lake of Memories after having viewed the Tooth Fairy's latest victim. Her name was Angelique Freeman, a black female in her early twenties from Milledgeville, Georgia. She had been attending college on the city's Northside when she disappeared. Like the others, Angelique was found bled dry, dressed in a white linen gown, her body weighted down by two cement-filled coffee cans. She had deep rope burns on her neck and was missing her two front teeth. Seeing her, Nation thought of his sister, Emma. Emma was twenty years old, attending college in New York, when the police dragged her body out of the Central Park Lagoon.

When the Tooth Fairy case went cold later in the summer, so did his career trajectory. But he wasn't haunted because he had made the overconfident statement or because he had egg on his face for failing to deliver. The thing that tortured his soul was the knowledge that the killer was still out there.

The following summer, Jones began receiving parcels, one about every two months, mailed to his attention at the U.S. Marshals District Office in Chicago. Each package contained a piece of a tooth carefully wrapped in the Town Journal headline, "I GUARAN-F******-TEE IT!" Each package was postmarked from one of the victim's hometowns, all but Milledgeville, Georgia.

About six months after the last package, the sixth parcel arrived, and as he expected, it was post-marked from Milledgeville. Jones put on gloves, carried the small box down to the lab, and opened it, careful to preserve anything of evidentiary value. To his surprise, this parcel contained two teeth. Why two teeth, he wondered? He'd never received two teeth before. One tooth was wrapped in the regrettable headline; the other taped to a postcard from Laconia, New Hampshire. The card featured a Rockwellian rendering of Main Street complete with a Woolworth, turn of the century automobiles, and children playing fetch with a small brown and white dog. Jones rushed back to his desk and initiated a search for reported missing subjects out of Laconia. Patricia Weintraub had been attending school in Denver, Colorado, at the time she went missing. Jones received four more teeth over the next ten months, and then nothing.

That had been five years ago.

"Nation, are you there?"

Jones felt sick to his stomach. He'd asked to go out to Denver to assist in the search for the Tooth Fairy, but his request had been flatly denied. In fact, following his request, he was moved from the apprehension team to the prisoner transport team, the post he currently held.

"Yeah, I'm here. But I can tell you right now, Sabo, Crenshaw will stick my ass behind a desk...no, under," he corrected himself. "He will stick me under a desk if I ask to be assigned to your case."

"Then don't ask!"

"Are you crazy? That's why you always get into trouble. That's why the best homicide investigator I've ever known is a fucking college rent-a-cop. I still got over eighteen years before I can retire. I'm not losing my pension like your dumb ass."

"Come on, man, don't be a pussy. You know you want this son of a bitch. And besides, just think about the points you could score with your boss after what has it been?" The voice on the other end of the line went silent for a moment, and Jones could picture Sabo counting on his fingers. "Six years — after six years, you finally make good on your promise to catch the Tooth Fairy. How fucking cool would that be?"

"I don't give two shits about scoring points with

my boss. I just want to keep under the radar until I hit fifty."

"Nation, I really need you on this, brother."

Jones thought Sabo sounded desperate. It was disconcerting coming from him. "I don't know, man, I'm already going to get jammed up on this drug bust bullshit." He paused for a moment and came back on the line.

"Man, I just can't. I'm sorry."

"It's okay, Nation. I understand. Let's hope it's just a copycat or a coincidence. Hell, what was I thinking? I'm a campus cop. Shit, I'm not even allowed to carry between home and work. I'm sorry I bothered you, brother."

"No, it was good to hear from you. Maybe we can meet up in Des Moines sometime and hit a couple blues bars."

"Yeah, I'd really like that. Look, I gotta get going. I have to secure the scene while we wait for the evidence team to finish up. Fly low, brother."

"Right, talk to you."

The line went dead, and Jones sat with the receiver in his hand until the busy tone started blaring through the earpiece. He set the receiver in the cradle and jumped when it started ringing again.

"Sabo, I told you, man, I can't..."

"Jones, is that you?"

"D.D. Crenshaw, I'm sorry, sir, I thought you

were someone else."

"That's obvious. What the hell have you been doing? I've been trying to call you for five minutes straight."

"Sorry, I was on the phone."

"No shit, you were on the phone. I already knew that."

"Right, well—"

"Listen, Jones, you know I like you, son, and I put my ass on the line when I suggested you to head up prisoner transport because I believe in you, but you really shit the bed, buddy. The director chewed my ass for almost an hour, so guess what!"

Jones sat and listened, well, half listened, as the deputy director chewed his ear, but all he could think about was the missing girl. What if she were still alive? What if some cop could have saved Emma and didn't?

"And I gotta tell you, Jones; you really let me down but—"

"Sir, I gotta go."

The deputy director continued screaming into the phone. "Go? What do you mean g—"

Jones hung up the phone, grabbed his Stetson off the desk, and started down the hall. He had just reached the elevator when he heard his phone ringing again. Jones hit the call button for the elevator. The damned thing was taking forever.

Jones pushed open the door to the stairwell and started down the stairs. The heels of his boots echoed in the empty stairwell, sounding as though someone were following him.

Maybe it's the Tooth Fairy, he thought as he exited at the basement level and jumped into his car. Jones always kept a bag packed in his trunk. In his line of work, he never knew if he would have time to run home before the job took him to God-knows-where. So, instead of having to waste time stopping at his place, Jones could afford to grab another coffee at The Bicycle Union. He parked in the lot behind the coffee shop and made a call while waiting for his order.

"Sabo, it's Nation. I'm on my way, brother. I'll be there in four hours."

3

Chapter 3

Thursday, May 9, 2019
Tabor County, Iowa

As he crossed the Iowa River traveling south on Highway 63, Rodney Oehlerking's stomach tightened. He was a very careful driver and never exceeded the speed-limit. He glanced down at his speedometer, 45 on the button. So, why was he looking at flashing red-and-blue lights in his rearview mirror? He signaled and pulled off the highway at Avenue J. About a hundred feet up on the right, if he remembered correctly, was a heavily wooded frontage road that led down to the river. He had cause to visit the area about five years prior. There was an incident involving a small boy who was simply in the wrong place at the wrong time.

The memory made him shudder.

Rodney turned onto the frontage road, slowly reached into the map pocket on the side of his door, and wrapped his aching fingers around the worn wooden handle of his hatchet. He set the hatchet on his lap and was about to pull over and stop when the impatient sheriff's deputy sounded his air-horn. The blast made Rodney jump, sending the hatchet tumbling to the floor. A second blast and Rodney waved a hand of acknowledgment, then rolled to a stop. He sat perfectly still, face forward, both hands gripping the wheel as his mind ran through multiple scenarios. A sharp rap on the glass with the deputy's flashlight pulled Rodney back into the moment. He rolled down the window.

"Evenin' officer; what seems to be the problem?"

"License and registration, sir."

"Course, officer. Mind tellin' me why I'm bein' stopped?"

"Just a courtesy stop, sir. Your vehicle's registration is obstructed."

"Beg pardon?" Rodney said, a confused frown forming on his face.

"Your license plate on your rear bumper — it's covered in mud, sir." The deputy spoke slowly and deliberately, as if to a child.

"Well, I do apologize. I'll be sure and take care of that."

"I'm sure you will, but I still need to see your license and registration."

"Course." Rodney held both hands up and shrugged meekly before slowly reaching into his glove compartment.

"Insurance too, sir."

"Certainly, officer," Rodney said cheerily as he fished his registration and insurance cards from under a pile of gas receipts. "Here you are, sir." He handed the cards to the deputy.

"License too, Mr..." The deputy redirected the glare of the light from the side of Rodney's face to the documents. "Oehlerking," the deputy finished.

Rodney handed his driver's license over and glanced down at the floorboard, making sure the hatchet wasn't visible. The deputy looked young. Rodney guessed he was in his early twenties, a rookie. Who else but a rookie would have stopped an old white man driving a beater car for having dirty plates in rural Iowa?

"Would you happen to have an old rag in your trunk, sir?"

Rodney's stomach dropped, and he felt his sphincter tighten. The object of his desire was in the trunk, and there was no way the deputy would let him leave with it. "Couldn't rightly say, officer," Rodney answered and licked his lips.

"It's deputy, sir. Deputy Robert Lawson."

"That's fortuitous."

"Fortuitous?"

"Yes, fortunate. A fortunate occurrence."

"I know what fortuitous means, sir."

"Of course. Well, I just mean to say, your surname has the word law in it, and you are a lawman."

"Right. So, what do you say we take a look in your trunk for a rag?"

"That won't be necessary, deputy."

"I'll be the judge of what is or isn't necessary, Mr. Oehlerking."

It was clear to Rodney that the young deputy did not like to have his authority questioned, and Rodney chose his next words carefully. "Course, Deputy Lawson, I simply meant that I can use the sleeve of my jacket to wipe off the mud." He opened his car door to step out.

Perhaps the deputy knew something. Then again, maybe it was just nerves; Rodney wasn't sure. Deputy Lawson's hand flew to his gun, his thumb unsnapping the holster as it passed. The beam of the deputy's flashlight pinned Rodney to his seat.

"Stop right there and keep your hands where I can see them!"

He hoped the deputy was just nervous. After all, it was a deserted road, and he seemed awfully young. Besides, how could the deputy know his secret? Rodney had been extra careful to avoid being seen.

Regardless, he did as he was told. Rodney threw his hands in the air and swallowed hard for effect. He considered going for his hatchet, but there was no way that he could grab it and strike Lawson before the deputy could put two rounds into the side of his head. The stream of light danced herky-jerky around the inside of Rodney's car, and he could tell that Lawson's hand was shaking.

"Officer," he said, in as calming a voice as he could manage.

"Deputy!" the lawman snapped. "Deputy Lawson."

"Beg pardon," Rodney paused. "Deputy Lawson, I meant no disrespect. I was under the impression that you wanted me to clean the mud off my license plate."

"What I want is for you to sit perfectly still!"

"Course, Deputy Lawson. As you wish."

Rodney watched out of the corner of his eye as the deputy's left hand went toward his lapel mic and then back down to retrain the light on the car's interior. It wasn't quite dark yet, but Rodney had parked in the shade of high trees, which cast his car in shadows. Rodney watched as the deputy repeated the back-and-forth motion several times; the young man was in a pickle, wanting to call for backup, but not wanting to take the light off of his detainee. Rodney felt a tinge of sympathy for the deputy, but it was short-lived as his instinct for self-preservation pushed pity aside. This had to be about more than a dirty license plate. Someone must have seen him and called it in. A trickle of sweat ran down the side of Rodney's face. He couldn't see Deputy Lawson's right hand, but he was fairly certain that the deputy's right hand held his service weapon, and the barrel was pointed right at him.

"Shut the car off, sir," commanded Lawson.

Rodney nodded meekly and did as he was told. The engine chugged and knocked a couple of times and went silent. He didn't realize the engine was so deafening until it quieted.

"Now, I want you to hand me the keys, slowly," Deputy Lawson ordered.

Rodney forced a tremble in his right hand for the deputy's benefit as he reached for the keys. As he drew the keys from the ignition, he let them fall to the floor. Rodney threw his hands into the air as quickly as he could.

"Sorry. I'm just so nervous. I've only been stopped once before, when I was a much younger man."

Rodney's false display of nerves seemed to calm the young deputy, whose voice took on a softer tone. "It's okay, sir. I'm going to need you to retrieve your keys from the floor slowly and hand them to me."

"I'm so sorry, deputy. It's just this damned body of mine. Riddled with this arthritis." Rodney held out his swollen knuckles for the deputy to see. "From my hands to my feet, son. But being a healthy young man, you probably don't know much about that."

"Actually, sir, I do. My father suffers from rheumatoid arthritis."

Rodney did his best to appear frail.

The deputy's demeanor had changed. He'd gone from authoritative to almost compassionate. "Let me help you with that, sir."

Rodney held up his left hand and bent with his right hand, searching the floor. "Thank you, son, but I think I can manage."

In a flash that rivaled the deputy's own reflexes, Rodney swung the hatchet in a short, tight arc, catching the deputy's right hand between the knuckles of his ring and middle fingers, severing tendons and small bones. Rodney sprung from his car like a large predatory cat and brought the hatchet down again, this time right across the deputy's stunned face. The razor-sharp blade split through the cartilage in the deputy's nose and sunk into his left eye. Rodney chopped and hacked until the young lawman was unrecognizable. Deputy Lawson coughed and sprayed blood from the pulpy mass that was once the face his mother loved, and then he was no more.

Rodney was wheezing, and he tugged at the front of his trousers, surprised to find that he had the beginnings of an erection. He stooped and wiped the blade of his hatchet across the deputy's pant leg. Rodney stood and stretched his back and then grabbed hold of Lawson's vest and began dragging the five-foot-eight, 245-pound body deep into the woods. Air whistled in and out of his dry throat as he set his feet and dragged, set his feet and dragged, set his feet and dragged. When Rodney had gone nearly half a mile, having worked for every inch, he stopped and caught his breath. Then, before heading back to the road, he made a deep cut across the deputy's gut with his hatchet. Rodney hoped that the smell would encourage woodland creatures to come and feast on the fat cop.

Rodney then hiked back out to the road where Deputy Lawson's Tabor County Ford Explorer police cruiser sat with its blinding overhead lights flashing. Rodney kicked loose dirt over Lawson's spilled blood and then picked up his license and registration before getting into the cruiser. The river was only about a half-mile up the road, but there was no way it would be deep enough to hide the deputy's SUV.

Things had been moving too fast for Rodney. He needed a moment to think this through. He pushed up his jacket sleeve, pulled his hatchet from his belt, and cut a small slash into his horribly marred forearm. The pain, he had found, helped clear his head and set the lesson firmly in his mind.

"Shoulda checked the damned car before I left," he groaned as he cut.

Rodney watched the blood drip from the slash and knew he wouldn't make that mistake again.

"Should have loaded the deputy's body into the cruiser instead of wasting all that time dragging him into the woods." Another tally-mark to his arm.

The pain was sobering, and that was good, because he needed a clear head. Rodney knew that a deep retention pond lay off in the woods on his left, but there was no way he could worm the SUV through the trees to get to it. There was a road that would take him right to its southern edge, but he would have to drive the deputy's cruiser back out onto Avenue J to get to it. Rodney looked at the gashes on his forearm and shit-canned that idea before it took root. Suddenly, he remembered the dirt path that snaked its way from the river back to the retention pond. If it were still there, it might be wide enough for the cruiser to pass. Rodney looked at the numerous switches and buttons, trying to figure out how to shut off the lights without accidentally hitting the air horn. A switch marked

0-1-2-3 sat in the second position. Hesitantly, he placed a finger on the switch and clicked it all the way to the left. The flashing stopped, and Rodney sighed in relief. He slipped the transmission into drive and drove to the river's edge. A man in a kayak headed toward the train bridge, waved as the Tabor County cruiser rolled slowly over the gravel. Rodney didn't bother to wave back. He found the path and followed it back to the clearing.

The retention pond was about thirty feet deep. In the summer, it was full of kids trying to beat the heat, but now, it was desolate. It was the perfect place to hide his sin. He pointed the cruiser at the pond, got the speed up to twenty, and rolled out. The tumble was hard, but he didn't think he'd broken anything. Carefully, Rodney moved into a sitting position and stared in disbelief. The front half of the Tabor County cruiser dipped over the edge and stopped. The car had gotten hung up on its undercarriage. Rodney walked over to the car and tried to lift the back end, but, strong as he was, he couldn't budge the cruiser.

He needed leverage. Rodney opened the rear hatch and began tearing through the contents: traffic cones, fire extinguishers, road flares. A myriad of crap littered the ground, but nothing useful. In frustration, Rodney picked up the first aid kit and slammed it against the back seat. The hard plastic box bounced off the seat and struck the interior wall, causing the third-row cup holder to pop off. There, down in the hole, Rodney found the jack he was looking for. He stacked all the crap from the trunk beneath the jack and cranked the bottle-jack to its highest position. When it stopped, he carried rocks over and placed them under the rear tires to hold the cruiser in position as he built up the support under the jack. The work was exhausting and took the better part of an hour, but Rodney finally succeeded in dropping the cruiser into the pond. With that finished, he trekked back to his car and was just about to get in when he heard a small voice.

"Hey, mister, are you okay?"

The boy was maybe nine years old. He sat on his bike with a fishing pole tied to the frame.

"What's that?" Rodney called back.

"You okay, mister?"

"Sorry, son, I'm a little hard of hearing." Rodney stepped away from his car and moved closer to the boy.

The boy repeated himself and placed a foot on his pedal.

"Oh," said Rodney. "I'm just fine, son. Had to take a pee."

The boy laughed. "I pee in the woods all the time."

"That's what they're for, son."

"That's not what my mom says."

"How's about we don't mention it to her then. What do you say?"

"Sure, mister, sounds good to me."

Rodney stepped closer. "That's a good boy. Catch anything?"

"Just a couple of mooneyes, about—" He held his fingers about eight inches apart. "—but I threw 'em back."

"You're quite the little fisherman," Rodney said. The boy was almost within arm's reach.

"Jeez, mister, what happened to your face?"

Rodney raised a hand to his cheek, remembering the unfortunate incident from his youth.

"You ever see a boar, you run the other way, boy." He ran his fingers over the smooth welts of his healed flesh. "Want to feel it?" he asked the boy and stepped closer.

The boy reached out his hand when a shrill whistle sounded in the distance.

"That's my mom, I better get going," he said, and shoved off hard on his bike, just as Rodney lunged for him.

$$4$$

Chapter 4

Friday, May 10, 2019
Cedar Falls, Iowa

S trips of bright yellow crime scene tape danced on the gentle evening breeze and drew looky-loos like flies to honey. Jones killed the engine and sat in his car, questioning his decision to get mixed up in yet another unofficial case. He knew that no matter the outcome, Crenshaw would have his ass when he found out. But he'd still taken precautions. Before leaving, he'd put himself out-of-office for the rest of the week and left his work cell in his desk drawer. The timing couldn't have been better; he didn't have any scheduled prisoner transports for the week, and he was sure Crenshaw felt like he got his two-cents in before the hang-up. Still, when you've stepped on your own dick as many times as he had, any veering from routine came with a side-order of dread, deep, abiding dread. Jones inhaled and blew out hard. "Here we go, dummy," he said to himself.

He set his U.S. Marshal's parking placard onto his dash to save the aggravation of a parking ticket, but then thought better of it and tossed it back into his glove box. No sense in advertising that he was there. Jones climbed out of his car and started for the campus security officer stationed near the door when his phone rang. He looked at the screen.

"Sabo, I just got on campus. Where are you?"

"Turn around, dip-shit."

Across the quad, Jones saw his old friend waving like he was greeting a friend in an airport.

"You can stop, I see you."

"Damn! It's good to see you," Sabo called as he approached. "When did you get so friggin fat?"

The two shook hands and hugged like old friends.

"Shit! You look old! Are you feeling okay?"

Sabo pushed Jones away. "Look who's talking!"

"It's good to see you, Sabo."

"You too, brother. Look, man, I'm sorry for dragging you all the way out here, but I need your help."

Jones dismissed the apology with a wave of his hand. "What can you tell me about our missing?"

Sabo glanced around. "Not here. Let's go grab a beer."

Jones looked at his watch. "It's not even noon."

"That's okay, let's take your car."

"Shouldn't we at least walk the crime scene?"

"We can't. The locals still have it locked down. Besides, there's nothing to see there."

"What do you mean, nothing to see?

"I mean nothing, as in nada. City P.D. has already bagged everything worth seeing, which wasn't much. Come on, man, let's grab that beer."

Jones rolled his eyes.

"Fine," Sabo said. "I'll have a beer. You can have coffee or whatever you pussy U.S. Marshals drink.

The two climbed into Jones's car, and in between sending text messages, Sabo directed him a few blocks off campus to a place called St. Elmo's. The place smelled of booze, cigarettes, and fried food. It was a true townie bar, a place where real people with boring faces could drink without the distractions of loud music and tight-bodied coeds dry-humping on the dance floor. Sabo led Jones through the dimly lit bar to a booth in the back and signaled for the waitress. Jones was surprised to find that the place was about half-full.

"Your kind of people."

"Yeah, yeah," Sabo said dismissively. "Look, I know it's been a while, but you and me, we've always been close. And I meant to call a bunch of times, but... well, you know."

"Yeah, I know. So what's with all the secret squirrel shit?"

Sabo looked around, leaned in closer, and lowered his voice. "It happened so fast. I just wasn't thinking." He dropped his head in his hands.

Thoughts raced through Jones's mind. "What are you talking about? What happened so fast?" That familiar feeling of dread crept up from his gut. "What the fuck did you do, Sabo?"

Sabo's eyes darted around the bar. "Shh! Keep it down, dude." Sabo fished around in the pocket of his jeans and pulled out a small black thumb drive.

"What's that?"

"It's a thumb drive."

"No shit, it's a thumb drive." Jones was losing his patience. "What's on it?"

Sabo swallowed hard, and his throat clicked. "It's... you know, the abduction."

Jones's eyes flashed. "The abduction?" He sat bolt upright and ran a hand across his forehead. "Are you telling me we may finally have a picture of the Tooth Fairy?"

Jones reached for the drive, but Sabo shoved it deep into his pocket.

"Sabo, what the fuck?"

"There's something I have to tell you."

The excitement fell as quickly as it had risen. "What is it?"

"It's about the girl... I knew her."

Jones threw his head back and stared at the ceiling. "Oh, for fuck's sake, don't tell me you were screwing her!"

"What? No, nothing like that! Jeez, what do you take me for?"

"You want me to answer that?"

Sabo made a face that Jones read as hurt feelings, but he didn't give two shits about hurt feelings. "So, what is it then?"

"I copied the video and scrubbed the machine."

Jones flew to his feet, causing a few heads to turn in the bar. "You what?"

Sabo glanced around nervously, pasted a smile onto his face for the other patrons, and whispered harshly, "Would you sit the fuck down?"

Jones looked around. He was drawing attention to himself, and that was the last thing he wanted, so he lowered himself back into the booth. "You better start talking, or I'm gonna leave your ass right here and drive straight back to Omaha."

Sabo made sure the rest of the patrons had gone back to their business. He brought his hand to his mouth, as if covering his lips would somehow hide his embarrassment. "I'm in the video."

"Tell me I didn't just hear you say that you're in

the same surveillance video as the missing girl."

"I wish I could."

Jones tried to piece things together. "Wait, but you weren't screwing her, so what's the big deal? Why the fuck would you tamper with evidence?"

Sabo raised his eyes to meet his friend. "I sell weed to some of the kids on campus. Our missing — Seneca Campbell, she's one of my customers." Sabo broke eye contact. "I forgot all about the security cameras until the police requested that we check our surveillance system."

Jones dropped his head into his hands. "You've gotta be fucking kidding me!"

"Dude, I panicked. Do you know what would happen to me if this got out? I'd be in lockup before dinner."

"For selling weed?" Jones challenged.

"Do you remember Jamie Mason?"

"Who the hell is Jamie Mason?"

"Congressman, Jamie Mason?"

"Shit, Sabo, I don't know the guy."

"Well, he used to be the mayor of Davenport."

Jones rolled his eyes and exhaled in exasperation. "You have got to be shitting me!"

"I shit you not."

"Well, maybe you shouldn't have fucked the guy's wife."

"I didn't — look, be that as it may, there are still a

bunch of dudes I put away that would give anything to stick a shiv in my back."

"Shit," Jones rubbed his forehead. You really are a piece of work."

"I know, and I'm sorry. But like I said, I really need you on this one."

"So, your number — it's going to show up on her call log?"

"What? No! I use a burner phone. You think I'm an idiot?" The look on Jones's face conveyed his thoughts. "Scratch that. Obviously, I'm an idiot, but I'm not stupid."

"Oh, you are way beyond stupid. You're screwed, and if you think you're dragging me down the shitter with you, you got another thing coming." Jones stood. "Thanks for the beer. Call me in another two years."

He turned to leave, but a short, broad-shouldered woman blocked his egress. He was about to sidestep her when she stuck out a hand.

"You must be National Jones."

More out of habit than congeniality, Jones shook her outstretched hand. "And you are?"

"Charlotte Rittenhouse, I'm a detective with Cedar Falls P.D. I'm assigned to the Major Crimes task-force. I understand that you're assisting with my investigation."

Jones shot Sabo a look. "I'm not assisting with

anything. In fact, I was just leaving."

"I see you have worked with Sabo before. Can't say I blame you for wanting to distance yourself."

Jones liked her already. "How did you even know we were here?"

"He sent me a text message. Said he got the great National Jones to help out with our case."

"Consult," Sabo corrected. "I said you were going to consult on our case. Now will you two please sit down?"

Charlotte slid into the booth and swept an inviting hand across the seat. Jones hesitated for a moment, then sighed sharply and joined her.

"How much has our friend told you?" Jones asked.

"You mean, has he told me about the thumb drive? Yes."

"And that he scrubbed the machine and withheld evidence?"

"He did, and I might arrest him myself once this is all done."

"So, wait, you're willing to risk your career and criminal charges to help this asshole?"

"Marshal Jones, I'm willing to do almost anything if it means stopping this bastard from murdering another young woman."

That quieted Jones. Charlotte reached into the messenger bag she'd been carrying and pulled out a small notebook computer. "Give it here, jackass," she said, extending a hand.

Sabo dug into his pocket again and handed the thumb drive to Charlotte. She plugged in the drive, and the gritty-looking black-and-white surveillance video popped onto her screen.

5

Chapter 5

Thursday, May 9, 2019
Oehlerking Farm – Rural Iowa

Ray Borowski was exhausted. The young bluesman from Bozeman Montana had spent the last week walking and thumbing his way across the Great Plains on his pilgrimage to Chicago, the Home of the Blues. The son of a wealthy cattle rancher, Ray knew very little of life's struggles and took great pride in the hardships he'd faced this past week. Bumming food and smokes outside gas stations, banging out tunes on his old Gibson Archtop for nickels and dimes, and working the odd job here and there in exchange for a place where he could lay his head for the night—be it a cot in the back of a bar or a bale of hay in a barn.

Ray was making his bones. It wasn't a deep pond of pain and suffering, but it was the best he could manage. And though he cherished the few trials and tribulations he'd faced, hell, he already had the workings of several good songs. The one thing he simply couldn't abide was the rain, and it was coming. It wasn't that he hated rain; as a child he would jump in the biggest puddles he could find on the ranch. It was just that he carried all of his worldly possessions with him and none of it was waterproof, least of all his guitar. So far, he had been lucky and stayed ahead of the storm that had been chasing him since a long-haul trucker had dropped him off in the little town of Gilman, about fifteen miles west of where he now stood. But Ray's luck was running out.

With the wind at his back and the smell of the wet earth sweeping into his nostrils, Ray stood at the end of a long gravel driveway staring at a house that couldn't have looked less inviting if it had been wrapped in barbed wire. He'd only passed three other houses on his long walk from Gilman, and he'd been turned away from all of them—one of them at gunpoint. Compared to what he now faced, however, that place looked like a Red Cross Station. But Ray was dog-tired. The sun had not yet gone down and storm clouds hung in the sky to the west—but the area around this place looked, to

Ray's mind anyway, darker than it should have.

"Beggars can't be choosers," he muttered as he dragged his weary bones up the driveway to the rotting old house.

The windows were dark and caked with dirt, giving the impression that no one was home. He took hold of the railing on the front steps, careful not to put his hand on the black mold that crawled its way from the underside, and stepped up onto the porch. He made sure to avoid the broken planks as he approached the door and raised his knuckles to give it a knock. His hand stopped mid-swing. Next to the door, a corn knife stuck out of a section of tree trunk that had been called into service as a chopping block. Such things were commonplace on farms and ranches, and he wouldn't have paid it any mind except that it was covered in a milky mass of maggots that throbbed and pulsed as it gorged itself on the blood that had soaked into the wood.

"What the hell kind of Deliverance shit is this?"

With his hand hanging in dead space, a crack of thunder peeled and Ray's hand flew forward, landing with a solid thud against the blistered paint of the heavy wooden door. Ray winced and watched with one eye closed tight as he braced himself for whatever banjo-toting half-wit emerged.

After a moment, Ray knocked again. As he stood waiting, he got the feeling that he was being watched. Lightning ripped the sky and thunder shook the porch beneath his feet.

"I think I just peed a little," he said to no one in particular, but it made him feel better to hear his own voice.

Again, there was no answer, so Ray took a seat on the porch step and broke out his guitar to wait for the homeowner to return. He gave a quick check to make sure it was in tune, though he didn't know why he bothered; the L-50 Archtop was always in tune, and he began to play. As he picked out the notes and chords to Bessie Smith's "Haunted House Blues," the wind picked up and thunder rolled. Ray "Bones" Borowski was reborn as a true bluesman. He sang and howled at the top of his lungs, fearing no ghost or goblin that might come calling. He'd played that song, and many others, hundreds of times, but this time was different. The music was alive inside of him.

When Ray struck the final chord, the old Gibson hollow-body resonated with nature herself and something deep inside his soul stirred. Like a man waking from a drowning nightmare, he struggled to catch his breath. He looked at his hands and touched his fingers to his throat. Ray was a good guitar player. Hell, he was better than good— anyone with ears could tell you that, but it never came naturally to him. He'd spent four hours a day, seven days a week for the past three years honing his skills in the loft in one of the barns on his parent's property where no one could hear him. When he finally played for his family, his mother said that he was like a human jukebox. He could mimic anybody, from Charley Patton to Lonnie Johnson, from Big Bill Broonzy to the late great Stevie Ray Vaughn. Ray Borowski could play it all, but he always sounded like a guy imitating some other guy. But there on that porch, something changed. Ray had found his own voice: rough, ferocious, incredibly liberating. And he couldn't wait for the rest of the world to hear it. He set his guitar in its case and snapped it shut. He bounced to his feet and howled like a wolf—then he noticed something in his hands, something he hadn't felt before. There was an ache in his knuckles, deep down in the joints. He rubbed them, but it didn't seem to help.

"Fucking weather. Messing up my fingers."

In a bold move, totally unlike himself, Ray turned toward the door, grabbed the knob, and gave it a twist. It didn't budge. Dejected, Ray Borowski turned to pack up his shit and hit the bricks. That was when he heard the voice for the first time— the one that he would come to know as Bones. And although he knew it was only in his head, it wasn't the voice of his normal inner dialogue.

"Slow your roll baby. Can't no lock stop a driven man."

Ray looked over at the corn knife. He grabbed the handle, not bothering to knock the maggots off. He felt their soft, wet bodies squish between his fingers. Undaunted, he forced the blade into the door jam and pried hard. Pain exploded in his shoulder and radiated through his body, but the lock gave way. He was about to scream out when he saw the headlights turn up the driveway from the old dirt road.

***

It had been a long day, but he finally made it. Rodney killed the engine and got out of his car. He stood a moment—his legs and back were stiff from the long drive—and then crossed over to his porch. The banister was worn and familiar, and it welcomed him home. He climbed the three steps to the landing and froze in his tracks. The front door stood open just a crack. He spun on his heels to make sure no one was coming up on him from behind, but all was quiet. Rodney placed his hand on the door and closed his eyes. He was sure the intruder was still there.

He drew his axe from his belt, slowly pushed the door open, and stepped inside. Before continuing into the house to search for the intruder, he shut the door, flipped the thumb-turn, and set the deadbolt in place with a satisfying thud. No one was getting out without answering for their trespass. With the door secured, Rodney moved into his bedroom to check on his treasure. The bed looked undisturbed and he almost breathed a sigh of relief when a thought occurred to him.

Perhaps the thief stole his treasure and then put the bed back in place so that it wouldn't be noticed.

Rodney dropped painfully to the floor and shoved the bed aside. He set the axe down and pried up the slat with his fingernails. In his haste, he bent one of his nails back and winced but continued removing the board. Slowly—he had to do this next part slowly. Rodney reached down inside and brought up his box. He held his breath as he lifted the top; his treasure was safe. He admired it for a moment and then returned it to its hiding spot.

With the box safely stowed away, he replaced the plank, returned the bed to its proper place, and got back to his feet, axe in hand. Rodney stalked his way through the rest of the rooms on the first floor. Satisfied that the bathroom, parlor, and kitchen, were all clear of any hiding burglar, Rodney walked over to the narrow staircase that led to the second floor. He rarely made the trek up the stairs; only when absolutely necessary, and this certainly qualified. Each step on the narrow staircase responded to Rodney's weight with a loud creak. Along with being narrow, the stairs were steep and shallow, and Rodney had to place his feet carefully. Up he went, step by step, until he reached the landing. The second floor was dark and Rodney flipped the switch on the wall at the top of the stairs. The lights flickered as they always did. Rodney exhaled in exasperation.

It was almost 8 PM, and the sun had begun its descent. Rodney stood at the head of the stairs, straining to see down the hall in the periodic flashes from the naked bulbs that hung from the ceiling. There were four rooms and a small bathroom, and Rodney knew he had to check them all. He moved to the first door, pulled a stick-match from his pocket, and struck it before entering the room. Like the first floor, the wallpaper was faded and peeling. This had been his mother's sewing room.

Rodney loved his mother and did his best to pre-serve it in a way that would remind him of her. The Singer model 66 Redeye sat in the corner, thread still in the bobbin, white linen material draped over the bedplate onto the floor. A torso mannequin that his father made for her out of bailing wire and rags sat in the other corner. Sometimes, as a boy, he would wait until he was sure everyone was asleep and then sneak into the sewing room and touch the mannequin. Rodney smiled at the thought and felt a familiar stirring, and then refocused on the job at hand. There was a chair by the door where he would sit and watch her sew and try on the dresses she made. Next to his chair was the dressing mirror, the glass fractured in one of his father's rages.

As the flame neared his fingers, Rodney blew it out and struck another match before he walked out into the hall. The next room was his parent's bedroom. Most of the room was occupied by their huge four-post-bed. His mother saw one in the Sears catalog and thought it was the most beautiful thing she'd ever laid eyes upon. Henry Oehlerking couldn't afford to buy her the things that he felt she deserved, but poor as he was, Henry was a talented craftsman. He took down the largest oak tree on their property and built her a bed that put the one in the catalog to shame. Rodney supposed that the bed would still be standing when the rest of the house collapsed. He looked up at the yellowing cracks in the ceiling and wondered why it was taking so long.

Along the east wall there sat a long dresser, which Henry had traded for two fat hogs. Rodney passed it and checked the closet. Still full of his parents' clothes, he took special care with his stick-match. Satisfied that the intruder was not in his mother and father's room, Rodney moved to the next door.

He struck another match and stepped into his childhood bedroom, where a flood of memories washed over him. The place where his bed once stood was vacant, having been moved down to the parlor, but the rest of the room remained just as it had been when he was a boy. The faded Iowa Hawkeyes pennant, which he had waived triumphantly over his head as his father carried him out of Kinnick Stadium on his ninth birthday, hung by rusty thumbtacks on his closet door. And though countless sunsets had scraped most of the color from the pennant, they couldn't dull the memory of that special day. Henry Oehlerking had been a hard man, leaving Rodney with very few warm memories of his father. So he locked those memories, precious and few, away in his mind— the only thing in his world that seemed immune to entropy.

On the wall next to where his bed had once been, a young Rodney had taped up two pictures from a coloring book he'd received as his only present one Christmas Morning. He'd selected those two because he had managed to stay within the lines, quite an accomplishment for a boy of six, made all the more special by the praise he'd received from his father. But those memories fell to pieces as his eyes came upon the little work desk that sat dust-covered and facing the corner. His father put it there when he was four. It was one of the ways Henry would punish and teach Rodney at the same time. Henry would make his son sit at that desk for hours at a time, copying scripture over and over until his hand cramped and his back ached. The memory was miserable but bad as it was, it was mild penance compared to—the *other* room. Rodney closed his eyes and shuddered at the thought as he stepped back into the hall.

Just one more room to check. He approached the door and placed a hand on the knob, but he didn't open the door. Rodney's stomach lurched and his hand began to tremble. The trembling spread from his hands to his legs and then to the rest of his body and he broke into a cold sweat. It was a solid minute before he realized it, but Rodney had been digging the blade of the axe into his leg. The warm blood spilled down his leg as he dropped his head and turned for the stairs. The *other* room would go unchecked.

Rodney walked down the narrow staircase and into his bathroom, where he dropped his pants and sat on the seatless toilet. The cut on his leg wasn't bad, but it would still require a couple of stitches. He reached across to the medicine cabinet and pulled a small tin box off the shelf. Rodney popped the box open and removed a rusted, curved needle and a spool of thread. He wiped the needle against his shirt and then struck another match to heat the tip. Once it began to glow red, he pressed it against the cut and waited for the sizzling sound to stop. He threaded the needle and passed it through his skin a few times, stitching the cut closed. Rodney pulled his pants back up, stowed the needle and thread, and limped out to his front porch.

6

Chapter 6

Friday, May 10, 2019
Cedar Falls, Iowa

Charlotte positioned the computer so that none of the other bar patrons could see it. A girl sat, legs spread, on one of the industrial dryers in the laundry room of Kobo Hall, the largest of the senior dorms on campus. Between the girl's legs stood a young man, his hands clamped tightly on her hips and his mouth pressed hard to hers in what looked to Jones like a face-eating contest. As they continued their frenzied display, the boy slid his hand up the girl's shirt. The young lady offered no resistance.

"You sure this is the right video?" Jones asked.

"Relax," Sabo said. "It's almost over."

After a few more seconds of what some might consider soft-core pornography, Jones watched as his old friend entered the frame. There was no audio, but he could see Sabo flailing his arms in the air and yelling. The two young lovers, not looking the least bit embarrassed, adjusted their clothing and walked off. As Jones watched, Sabo walked toward the camera and disappeared beneath the view of the lens.

"Assholes weren't even doing laundry," Sabo said, sounding almost self-righteous.

Jones rolled his eyes and continued to watch as a girl with a long blonde ponytail came into view.

"That's Seneca."

Charlotte pulled a file from her bag and compared the picture she'd obtained from the family to the girl on the screen. Seneca was smiling, and though there was no audio, it was obvious that she was speaking with Sabo.

"What is she saying?" Jones asked.

"Nothing, man, we were just doing the deal."

Jones's face soured. He couldn't have hidden his disgust even if he had wanted to. The exchange took only a moment and then Sabo left the room. Seneca pulled her cell phone from the pocket of her orange hoodie. Her ponytail had been hanging over her right shoulder, covering part of the word written across the zip-up.

"What does that say?" Jones asked.

"I don't know, all I can read is *cers*," Charlotte answered. "I wish she would..."

Almost as if Seneca could hear her, she whipped her ponytail off her shoulder.

Jones's face tightened. "Lancers. Why do I know that name?" Jones flipped open a note pad and began jotting.

Seneca's thumbs flew across the screen of her cell phone, but there was no way to see what she was typing. A second later, she put her phone to her ear and became highly animated. Seneca danced around as she spoke and then set her feet firmly on the ground and pointed down with her free hand. Jones read the pantomime.

"She just told someone she would be waiting right there for them."

"Agreed," Charlotte said.

Seneca stuck her phone back in her pocket, danced around for a few more minutes, and then stopped suddenly. She stood facing the camera and her expression changed. Even in the grainy black-and-white video, the terror on her face was unmistakable. Eyes wide with fear, her lips pulled back to show her teeth, some ancient response from the amygdala, Seneca backed herself into a corner. A tall, lanky figure wearing a dark jacket and a hat moved toward her.

"How tall is she?" Jones asked.

"Like five-two," Sabo answered. "Why?"

"Can you pause it?"

Charlotte hit the pause button and Jones pointed at the screen.

"He's over a foot taller than her. I'm guessing six-six. Not a lot of dudes that tall walking around," Jones said, and then followed with: "This school have a basketball team?"

"Yeah," Sabo answered.

"Why would she react that way to another student?" Charlotte asked.

"She hasn't filed any reports with campus security," Sabo said.

Jones rubbed his chin. "Sabo, how would you describe her build? It's hard to tell with the hoodie."

"She's tight," Sabo said. Then, reading the look of disgust on Charlotte's face, he added, "I mean, she's in really good shape. I think she used to be a gymnast. Why?"

"All of the Tooth Fairy's victims were college-aged females with small muscular frames and blonde hair. Even Angelique Freeman."

"Who's Angelique Freeman?" Sabo asked.

"I guaran-fucking-tee it," Charlotte said with a knowing smirk.

Jones sighed. "Yeah. Angelique was a black girl from Milledgeville, Georgia. She ran track. A week before Angelique was taken, the whole team dyed their hair blonde in tribute to a teammate who'd been killed in a crash on Lake Shore Drive. Like I said, the Tooth Fairy always takes small, athletic blondes."

"Fuck," Sabo said. "Still, though, why does Seneca look so scared?"

"Maybe he had a weapon?" Jones suggested.

"You can see his hands," Charlotte said. "There's no weapon."

"Maybe it's just because he's a stranger," Sabo suggested.

"No," said Charlotte. "People don't react that way to strangers."

"You've obviously never been black," Jones said, only half-kidding.

"Maybe he's wearing a mask or something?" Sabo offered.

"I don't think so," Jones said. "Can you hit play?"

Charlotte obliged.

"Then what?" Sabo asked.

As the video resumed, the figure continued toward the frightened co-ed and raised his hand in the air.

"Stop it right there!" Jones said.

Charlotte hit the pause button. "What do you see?"

Seneca had backed up against a wall of windows

that acted like mirrors against the darkness outside.

"There, in the glass, you can make out his face."

"Whoa," said Sabo.

Charlotte touched the screen. "That's why she's scared."

The flesh on the right side of his face looked like it had been boiled down and left to cool. Where his right eye should have been, there was only a small hole, about the size of half a dime; the flesh from his brow above hung like melted wax, covering the other half of the hole. The corner of his mouth was pinched shut, and where his right ear should have been was another hole, about the size of a number two pencil eraser. Thick ropes of scar tissue ran in cords down his neck.

"Holy shit," Sabo said.

"Holy shit is right," said Jones. "I think we have our first image of the Tooth Fairy."

Jones reached forward and hit play. Seneca launched herself off the wall to push past the man, but it was no use. His hands flew out and he snapped her up in a chokehold. Seneca thrashed for several seconds, and then her body went limp. Jones's jaw tightened and he clenched his fists.

"Motherfucker."

As they watched, the Tooth Fairy swept the girl up in his arms and laid her down on the laundry room's folding table. He brushed her bangs aside with his fingertips and then ran a hand slowly from her neck down her body, pausing momentarily at her breasts before he continued down to her stomach and her hips. He reached back toward her mouth and parted her lips and teeth.

Sabo cringed and turned away. "Aw, shit. He's gonna do it. He's going to take her teeth. I can't watch this."

"No, he's not," Jones said. "Not if it's really him. Mouth injuries make a lot of blood, and the Tooth Fairy never leaves blood."

Charlotte leaned in. "What else can you tell us about him?"

"I spent over two years hunting and studying the Tooth Fairy. He's a ritualistic, mission-oriented serial killer. He sees what he's doing as a calling. Probably thinks he's doing God's will. He grabs his victims from college campuses and parks—and in one case, a mall parking lot—then he takes them to a second location. We assume it's somewhere isolated. There, aside from doing God knows what to them, he removes their two upper incisors. Then he dresses them in white linen, binds them, and transports them to the dumpsite. Always in water because that's how he kills them. He weighs them down with cement-filled coffee cans, one at the neck and one at the feet, so that they lay flat and drops them into the water. The rope around the neck is tight enough to hold them under but not so tight as the victim can't breathe. After all he puts them through, he kills them by drowning."

"Water in the lungs?" Sabo asked.

Jones nodded, and Sabo took a breath, but Charlotte seemed unfazed. "Any indication of rape?"

"No, there's nothing to suggest that he's had sex with any of his victims," Jones said. "But the autopsies showed that all of his victims had been sexually active."

"Could he be punishing them?" Charlotte asked.

"Really can't say, though we never ruled it out. The thing is, there were never any injuries to their breasts or genitalia. The only indication of sadistic behavior is in the removal of the teeth."

"The method of death is consistent with my two, coffee cans, tied loosely around the neck, water in the lungs," Charlotte said. "Any thoughts regarding occupation? Maybe a traveling salesman?"

"We looked at that. Checked hotels and short-term rentals in all the cities where the Tooth Fairy had been active and came up empty. But I can tell you this—if he works at all, his job does not require employees to be fingerprinted. We've found prints at every dumpsite and on every letter he's sent to me. If his prints were on file anywhere, I would have had him behind bars years ago."

Charlotte hit play and the video resumed. Jones

was right—there was no taking of teeth, and there was no blood. The scarred man pulled what looked like a handkerchief from his jacket pocket and shoved it in Seneca's mouth. He then secured it with duct tape, lifted her onto his shoulder, and carried her out of the laundry room.

Jones's heart pounded in his chest. "We have to get that image out to the press. Someone is going to know a face like that."

"No!" Sabo protested. "I withheld evidence and scrubbed the hard drive. I'll lose my badge if that video gets out!"

Jones stared dumbfounded at his old friend.

"Oh, fuck you. Maybe I'm not some big Federal Marshal, but campus cops are police too."

"A girl's life is at stake here! And, newsflash, you're not campus police, you're campus security, dickhead, and you *should* lose your fucking badge. If this were my case, I'd charge you with obstruction! And you!" Jones turned his attention toward Charlotte. "How could you agree to keep this a secret?"

Charlotte threw up her hands. "Timeout, he just told me that he had some video he thought I should see. I didn't know he was withholding." She said, and directed her attention at Sabo. "He's right. We have to put this out."

One of the bar regulars, a guy in a too-tight black t-shirt with biceps like softballs, walked over. "We got a problem over here, Sabo?"

Jones set the muscle-bound man with a glare.

"No, Bobby, we're good. My buddy here is just a little upset."

"Well, just keep it down," he said and walked away.

The last thing Jones needed was to get into a bar fight. That would mean police, and police meant paperwork and a paper trail.

"Listen," Jones said, lowering his voice. "We have to get that image out. No ifs, ands, or buts."

Sabo's eyes darted around as if his gaze were turned inward and he was searching through file drawers in his mind. "What if we cut the tape and only put out the part with the Tooth Fairy on it?"

"Hell no," said Jones. "A defense attorney will challenge a cut tape, and no judge in the country would overrule it."

"You're right," Charlotte said. "But we don't have to make the whole tape available until trial. It's an open investigation. That means we control every piece of information that gets out, at least until we make an arrest and the Tooth Fairy hires an attorney."

Jones scratched the side of his neck. "Yeah, I suppose you have something."

"But I will have to seize that thumb drive and enter it into evidence with the rest of the stuff the evidence techs collected."

"It's going to cost me my job," said Sabo.

Jones clenched his fist and drew a deep breath. Sabo threw his hands up.

"But you're right. I'm a fuck up, and I don't deserve a badge."

If he was hoping for contradiction, he didn't get it. Charlotte snapped her laptop closed and pulled her ringing cell phone from her pocket.

***

Charlotte read the display. Tom Parnell. He was the head of Major Crimes, and he only called for two reasons: to demand an update on a hot case or to pile more shit on her already overflowing plate. She braced herself and hit accept.

"Charlotte Ritten—"

"I know who you are, I called you, remember?"

"Right, so what do you want, Tom?"

"Where are you?"

"I'm working a case."

"How fast can you get to Tabor County? Somewhere around—" He paused, and Charlotte could hear him rifling through papers. "Sixty-third and Avenue J. There's supposed to be an access road there that leads down to the river."

"Tom, I might have a break on our two dead girls. There's been another girl taken, and—"

"Look, you know I wouldn't be *ordering* you to do

74

this if it wasn't important. We got a dead cop who is missing and one still clinging to life."

Charlotte's face contorted. "Did you say—how do they know he's dead if they can't find him?"

"How the hell should I know? Just get your ass to Tabor County," he said and hung up.

"Son of a bitch," she murmured.

"What was that about?" Sabo asked.

"I don't know, sounds like a couple of officers got shot—or— shit, I don't know. He's such an asshole."

"Who?" Sabo asked.

"Tom Parnell, the director for the Northeast Major Crimes Unit."

"Were the officers on a call together, or are we talking about two separate incidents?" Jones asked.

"He didn't say. I doubt he even *thought* to ask." She let out a frustrated growl. "Look, I'll have to go down there and start sorting things out."

She clicked around on her keyboard and found the best view of the Tooth Fairy's reflection in the glass. Jones watched as she dragged a box around the image. Her fingers flew across the keys and she snapped the computer shut.

"Sabo, I just sent you a copy of the image we are going to use for the press release. Get it over to Reed Kelly at Channel 17. Tell him I sent you and we want that picture leading the next news cast." She locked eyes on Sabo to make sure he understood.

Sabo nodded and checked his phone. "Got it."

"Nation, I'm going to need you and Sabo to field calls in my absence. I don't want any going to my office. Every lead has to be documented and vetted before it gets forwarded to the investigators, and we don't have that kind of time."

"Agreed," Jones said. "But until we know for sure that it's really him, and we have him in custody, I don't want my name connected to this."

"Had enough egg on your face?" Sabo asked smugly.

Jones ignored him. "Look, if this really is the Tooth Fairy, I don't want him to feel like I'm challenging him."

"Why not?" Charlotte asked. "That might be the thing that makes him slip up."

"Or, it might be the thing that gets Seneca killed. I mean, if she's still alive."

"Nation's right," Sabo agreed.

"Fair enough." Charlotte slid her laptop into her bag and stood to leave. "I'll call you guys when I know what I have out there."

Charlotte walked out of the bar and shielded her eyes against the sun. She crossed the street and climbed into her unmarked Crown Vic. She'd nicknamed the car Bernie. Sometimes she said it was after the politician because it pulled so hard to the left: other times, she said it was after the movie where a couple of guys pretend their boss is still alive after a hitman kills him. Either way, the car was a piece of shit. Like all the cars in the detectives' pool, Bernie had already suffered a lifetime of abuse as part of her department's patrol fleet, and it deserved to be put out of its misery. But, when it came time to order new cars, there was never any room left in the budget for the detectives' cars. Charlotte sighed and turned the key. The engine objected at first, but after a couple of tries, it started up. She punched her destination into the GPS on her cell phone and set it in the cradle.

"An hour and a half, seventy-five miles, well fuck me," she said, and put Bernie in drive.

7

Chapter 7

Thursday, May 9, 2019
Oehlerking Farm – Rural Iowa

R ay "Bones" Borowski crouched behind the rusted shed and watched the lanky old man walk from his car toward the house. He could tell by the man's movement that walking was difficult, even painful. Ray frowned and rubbed at the soreness in his knuckles that seemed to be getting worse. As he watched the man struggle up the stairs, Ray was overcome by a feeling of guilt. He decided that he would fess-up and offer to fix whatever damage he had done to the door. Who knew, maybe the old guy would be appreciative of his honesty and offer him some food and a place to stay until the storm passed. Ray had just shifted his weight to the balls of his feet when the old man spun on his heels and pulled a hatchet from his belt. Ray couldn't make out his features in the dark, but could see him craning his neck and moving his head spasmodically, like a bird on the lookout for danger — or looking for prey.

Slowly, Ray slid back into the darkness behind the shed, careful not to make a sound. He didn't take his eyes off the old predator until he was closed up in the house. Once he heard the door close, Ray breathed a sigh of relief and gathered up his belongings. Rain or no rain, it was time to beat feet. He started down the driveway when he heard what sounded like a muffled scream. Instinctively his eyes shot toward the house and he froze, hoping against hope, that it had just been the wind howling. Then he heard it again and he knew it wasn't the wind. He also knew it hadn't come from the house. The scream came from the trunk of the old man's car.

"Mind your own binness, boy!"

He heard it clear as day, but when he looked around, there was no one there.

"Dammit, boy! You mind your own got-damned binness!"

It wasn't his voice, but there wasn't anyone else around. He looked back at the house, expecting to see the old man standing and waving his hatchet on the porch, but the door was still closed. After a couple of minutes, the lights flickered on the second floor and Ray took that to mean that he had time. But time for what?

"Time to run, dip-shit!"

The voice had a heavy southern twang. Ray still couldn't place it, but it seemed to be coming from inside him as well as all around him. Then he heard the sound of soft crying, and he knew *that* was coming from the trunk.

"Fuck! Hang on, I'm gonna get you out of there," he whispered as loudly as he dared.

Ray dropped his gear, ran to the trunk, and pulled on the lid. Naturally it wouldn't budge, so he hurried around to the driver's door, pulled it open and reached for the ignition.

"Fuck!"

No keys in the ignition. He flopped down the visor... nothing. Nothing under the floormat either. That was where they kept the keys to all the trucks on his dad's ranch and the shittiest one in the bunch was a hundred times better that this hunk of shit. When he left home, his father offered him a brand-new F-250 and a Gold Card, but Ray refused. No self-respecting bluesman could accept an offer like that.

A dim light glowed in one of the rooms on the second floor and then went out, and Ray was sure the guy was coming back down. In a last-ditch-effort, he jammed his hand under the front seat and began fishing around... nothing again. As he pulled his hand back out, he felt something pierce the top of his hand and rip into his flesh. Ray bit down hard on the pain and froze for a second. He couldn't see what had him, but he was pretty certain it was the rusty end of a seat coil-spring. Whatever it was, it had dug itself in good and deep, and sunk deeper each time he tugged to free himself.

"Motherfucker!"

Ray steeled himself for the agony, and in all likelihood, tetanus. For the briefest of moments, Ray tried to recall when he'd gotten his last booster. Then, gritting his teeth, Ray pushed forward for momentum and pulled back hard. His hand ripped free, and blood dripped warm and sticky between his fingers. He moved his fingers in a guitar-picking motion and breathed a slight sigh of relief as he realized his fingers still worked. As he considered his next move, the front door of the house flung open and banged hard against the side of the house.

***

Rodney stood on his porch and stared out into the electric night. He breathed in long and slow, smelling the ozone in the air. It wouldn't be long before the first drops began to fall, and Rodney welcomed it. The days leading up to big storms were always the worst. The steady drop in air pressure caused his already tender joint tissue to expand, pushing harder and harder against the shard-like crystals of uric acid in his body. Once the storm passed, he knew he would have some relief, but until then, his symptoms, and his mood, would only worsen. Rodney stepped down onto the first stair and stopped. His car door stood open and he was sure, just like with his house, that he had closed it.

"Somebody funnin' me?" His voice boomed over the thunder that peeled in the distance. His hand fell to his hatchet. "I don't like folks funnin' me." Rodney lowered his head and peered deeper into the darkness.

Pain or no pain, he leapt from the porch like a jungle cat and was on the car door in an instant. Nostrils flared, sucking in air like a jet engine; Rodney caught a scent. His dull, cloudy eyes, now sharp and clear, scanned the darkness and picked up the few drops of blood on the ground near the door.

"I'm gonna find you, and when I do…"

With his sharp eyes, Rodney looked for a blood trail but saw none. He sniffed wildly, like a police K-9 trying to pick up a scent, but the heavy smell of ozone left him with nothing to follow. He stopped momentarily at the trunk and heard the soft moaning from inside. He felt himself begin to go erect.

Snapping his head away, he drove thoughts of pleasure out of his mind and refocused on the work at hand. He moved toward the shed and spotted more droplets of blood. His lips parted into a yellow grin. He was getting close and he knew it. Rodney reached the shed and lifted the thick rubber cowling that protected the lock from the weather. The padlock was in place and the hasp was shut. He gave the lock a good hard tug just to be sure. Rodney re-gripped his hatchet, slowed his breathing and caught sight of a cracked branch and more blood disappearing behind the shed.

8

Chapter 8

Thursday, May 9, 2019
Tabor County, Iowa

Joanna Parks looked at her watch for the third time and cursed. Her sons were supposed to have been home an hour ago. She was a single parent, busting her ass to raise two boys on a dental hygienist's salary and whatever hours she picked up waitressing, but did they appreciate that? Hell, no! They couldn't even get their asses home when they were supposed to. She reached for her phone and braced herself for the call she knew she had to make.

"Shit," she said as she dialed the number to Prickly Pete's.

"Prickly Pete's," the voice on the other end of the phone said.

"Pete, it's Jo."

"Where the hell are you? Your shift started half an hour ago."

The place sounded busy; no surprise for a Thursday night. "I know, and I'm really sorry. The boys were supposed to be home by 5:30."

The owner, Prickly Pete Parsons, was a decent enough guy. He got a little handsy sometimes, but what else was new? Pete's was the place to be on Thursday nights. Every Tom, Dick, and Harry in the restaurant business had fish fries on Friday nights, but not Pete. Pete did his fish fry on Thursdays, and business was booming.

"Well, I'm sorry, but I'm gonna have to call Tracy in. I'm getting slammed over here!"

"Shit, come on, Pete. You know I need the money."

"Well, you ain't makin' shit sittin' at home."

"I know, Pete, but I'm worried." She wasn't worried. Her kids were selfish little assholes and never thought about anyone else, but the ploy worked.

"Look, I'll give you one more hour, then I'm calling Tracy. Gina and Jenny are up to their fucking eyeballs in fish and beer!"

"Thanks, Pete. I'll owe you one."

"Right," he said. "Just get your cute little ass down here!"

She hung up the phone, grabbed the pot of mac and cheese off the stove, and dumped the now-cold gelatinous blob into the garbage. "Sorry, boys," she said, speaking only to herself. "Dinners in the garbage. Bon appétit," she said and tossed the empty pot in the sink.

Billy Parks passed the joint to his little brother, whipped out his penis, and pissed descending arches across the face of the train bridge abutment. Joey Parks toked hard and coughed out blue smoke like a shitty old engine that burned too much oil.

"Holy crap, Billy..." His cough turned to a hack. "That's good shit."

Billy snatched the joint out of Joey's hand and punched him hard in the chest. "One for cough-ing!"

"Damn, man!" Joey rubbed the spot where his brother's fist had landed.

Billy jerked his fist back again, and Joey flinched. Billy punched him on the shoulder. "And that's two for flinching!"

Joey sucked air through his teeth and turned his back to his brother so he couldn't see the tears welling up in his eyes. That would be three for crying, and he sure as shit didn't want that. But it wasn't necessary. Billy had already started climbing up the grade to the train trestle above.

Joey pushed the pain aside and started after his brother. "Wait up, Billy!"

He was used to his brother hurting him. It had become so commonplace that he began to group and categorize the beatings according to size. In his mind, Joey would place each punch in a separate white box with a snug-fitting lid. Some of the boxes were relatively small, like the one-for-coughing and two-for-flinching variety. Others, like the ones that left bruises and black eyes, were a little bigger. Either way, he would box them up and drop the box over an imaginary edge into the pit of his stomach. He had once heard someone in a movie use the idiom. The guy said that he had a feeling in the pit of his stomach, and it made him sick, and something about that felt right. The beatings made Joey feel sick, so he figured a deep pit in his stomach would be the best place for those memories.

Over the years, Joey filled most of his pit with small boxes, and he was glad because sometimes the big boxes were hard to push over. A big brother wasn't supposed to hurt you; a big brother was supposed to protect you. He knew that because some of his friends had big brothers, and even though they busted their little brothers' balls, they never hurt them. No, Billy wasn't like the other kids' big brothers. There was something wrong with Billy. Something that made him want to hurt small things.

Joey shoved the new box over the edge and started up after his brother. He'd only gone up a few feet when the box finally hit the bottom of his pit, and in doing so, loosened the lid on one of the biggest boxes down there. The memory poked a spindly leg out from under the lid and crawled its way up from the pit like a dusty old spider. The spider crawled into his brain and laid an egg, and Joey froze, held in a trance, as it hatched.

It had been a hot June afternoon, about two weeks after school let out for the summer. Joey, Billy, and a bunch of other kids were hanging out on the basketball court near school. They'd spent the morning hunting butts on the sidewalks. Sometimes people would take a couple of drags off a cigarette and drop it on the ground, especially near the bus stops, and the kids had brought in a pretty good haul that morning. Billy always got first pick because, like Joey, all the other kids were afraid of him. Then, the rest of the group would grab what they could. That day, Billy grabbed his smoke and then offered the pile to Joey. Billy had put him ahead of the rest of the gang, and it made Joey feel warm inside — so good that he had forgotten his place. A mistake that would cost him.

The boys started talking about the MMA fight they had just seen. Ben Baker's dad said that Ben could invite a few friends over to watch the pay-per-view event, and naturally, Billy got an invitation. Their mom said that he couldn't go unless he took Joey. Joey was thrilled, but he was about to regret it. Ben was talking about how one fight ended in a submission because of a hold called an armbar.

"Once he had that guy in the armbar," Ben shouted, "I knew it was over."

In an uncharacteristic expression of bravado, likely brought about by his brother's act of kindness, Joey spoke up. "You're full of shit, Ben. Anyone can get out of an armbar. You just have to lock your hands."

None of them knew the first thing about mixed martial arts, but every time one fighter would try to get another fighter in an armbar, the announcers would always say that the guy better lock his hands.

"Not if the other guy is bigger than you," Ben challenged.

"Doesn't matter how big he is." Joey took a puff and blew it out. "You just have to not lose your grip." Joey passed his cigarette to one of the other kids. "Come on, I'll show you."

Ben and Joey were about the same size, and Joey felt confident he could take him. But then his brother spoke up.

"Ben's a scrawny little fuck, like you."

"I... I know Billy, I was just saying." The words caught in Joey's throat as Billy got to his feet.

"Let's go," Billy said, waving him out of the bleachers.

"Forget it, Billy. I was only kidding," Joey said, certain that his brother could smell the fear coming off him.

"Don't make me come get you."

The words slammed like a sledgehammer in Joey's head. He'd heard his father say them to his mother, and what followed was never good, especially if she didn't obey.

"Okay, Billy," he said, figuring he could just tap out like the fighter did.

Joey lay on his back and offered his arm to his brother.

"Lock your hands, dipshit."

Joey did as he was told, and Billy grabbed his little brother's wrist as he tried to apply the armbar. The small crowd of kids hooted and hollered. Joey's defense seemed to work. Joey could see Billy's face turning red, but held on tight. Then the thought of what it would cost him for embarrassing his brother popped into his head, and he lost his grip. Joey tapped immediately, but Billy didn't let up.

"Okay, Billy! I give; I give. I'm tapping out!"

Billy's lips squirmed their way into a wild grin.

Joey's arm was bent like a banana, and his brother showed no signs of stopping. The other kids stood around in a loose circle. Some, mostly the girls, turned away. They didn't want to see. Some pleaded with Billy to let him go.

"Come on, Billy, he tapped," said one kid.

"Yeah, Billy, let him go! He tapped," another agreed.

One kid even tried appealing to his own self-interest. "Billy, if you break his arm, your mom will kill you!" But Billy was disconnected; his information receiver had shut down. All of his energy, all of his focus, was on one thing. He breathed heavily and began sweating as he wrenched the arm. Joey looked up at his brother. What he saw froze his blood; Billy's bright blue eyes had turned into black eggs in their sockets. Billy torqued and didn't stop until Joey's elbow gave with a sickening pop. Joey screamed like a girl in a slasher movie.

Billy stood smiling at his brother's mangled arm. It was the most grotesque smile Joey had ever seen. When Joey looked into Billy's eyes, they were back to the brilliant blue people had always commented on. Slowly, the pain dulled into a deep throb.

Breathing heavily, Joey spoke through gritted teeth. "Shit, Billy, you broke my fucking arm, dude."

"Yeah, I did," he stated matter-of-factly.

"Why?" Joey rasped, pulling his arm to his chest, a fresh wave of pain spiking through his body.

Billy's smile folded into something that Joey read as confusion.

"Why?" he asked incredulously. "Because I wanted to know how it felt, dumbass."

Joey lifted his head and screamed at his brother. "It hurts like hell! What do you think?"

The confusion settled deeper on Billy's face. "Not for you, stupid. For me," he said as the smile twisted itself back onto his face.

"Hurry up, dipshit. Mom wanted us home by 5:30!"

The sound of Billy's voice snapped Joey out of his memory. Joey shuddered and wiped his sweaty palms against his jeans. That memory always made his palms sweat. Then he grabbed onto the vines that grew out of the side of the grade and started up after his brother. He'd made the climb up to the trestle a hundred times before, and he knew where to grab. About halfway up the climb, Joey looked up to see how close he was, and Billy flicked the roach at him from above. Joey jerked his head, and the hot cherry struck his cheek just below his right eye.

"Fucking Billy, man!" He knew his brother had been aiming for his eye.

"What did you say?" Billy locked him in his wild blue stare; the light brown curls in his hair danced gently on the breeze.

Joey froze, and his heart throbbed in his throat. He knew that look. If Billy so much as moved in his direction, Joey would slide down the hill and run for his life. He wouldn't stop running until he hit the Mississippi River, and then he would start swimming. He would run because he knew the reason Billy hadn't ever hurt him as badly as he had that one summer. It wasn't because he felt bad, or because he was sorry, or even because he was afraid that he would get into trouble. He hadn't done it again because he hadn't needed to. Joey knew he was nothing more than a lab rat to Billy, and he knew that one day, maybe one day soon, his brother would begin to wonder what it would feel like to kill someone, and that would be the day he died. Unless of course he got away in time.

"That's what I thought you said." And with that, it was over. The crisis had passed, and Billy started up the hill again.

Joey exhaled a sigh of relief and started back up after his brother. When he'd reached the top, he found Billy leaning against the fence rail, blowing smoke rings into the air. His tan shoulders were broad for a boy of fourteen; Billy Parks was one strong son-of-a-bitch. In contrast, Joey was thin, terribly thin, and always pale, except for the times he got sunburned. Then he would turn lobster red, blister, peel, and turn pasty white again. Looking at the two of them together, one would never guess that they were related, let alone brothers.

Mom said that Billy looked like his father. "The good-for-nothing piece of shit." She always said it as if it were his royal title or something.

"I'm glad neither of you turned out like your father, the good-for-nothing piece of shit." Or, "Your father left us without a pot to piss in, the good-for-nothing piece of shit."

Joey, on the other hand, looked like his mother. He shared her straight brown hair and delicate features. Joey had a small frame and no discernible muscle tone, but what he lacked in size and strength, he made up for with speed. He was jackrabbit fast and agile as a chimp.

"What the hell took you so long?"

Joey didn't answer, distracted by the thick smoke rings that floated up and away. "Cool! Can you teach me?"

Billy jetted smoke out of his nostrils. "Maybe later. We're already half an hour late," he said, jutting his chin toward the big clock on the grain elevator across the river. "We're gonna be in deep shit. Come on."

Billy took off running across the railroad ties, but Joey moved more carefully. Step, stop, step, stop, so as not to miss the wood and catch the gap.

He wasn't skinny enough to fall through, but he would tear up a shin, or worse, rack his balls if he missed. Billy stopped only once to spit at a kayaker on the Iowa River as he passed below. When they reached the other side of the bridge, they sat down on their butts and slid down on the two pieces of cardboard they'd left behind on their way to the other side. The slope, though gentler than the bridge's other side, still allowed for sliding. When they reached the bottom, Billy decided they should take the shortcut to make up time. Joey was dead set against it, but in the end, Billy got his way. Billy always got his way.

They'd only gone about a hundred yards into the woods when they heard a high-pitched buzzing sound. Then they saw it. Split open at the middle and swarming with flies, the body of a cop or maybe a security guard, Joey couldn't tell from where he was standing, and he didn't want to get any closer.

"Holy crap, Joey, you gotta see this!"

Joey had already seen more than he wanted to. "Come on, Billy, let's get out of here before we get in trouble." Strange that even in his panic at seeing a dead body, he understood the importance of appealing to Billy's sense of self-preservation. Joey watched unblinking as his brother ignored his plea and approached the body.

Billy squatted and ran his fingers over the

intestines that spilled from the gash across the deputy's torso, causing Joey to fight back the urge to puke.

"Feels kind of slimy and rubbery," Billy said as he continued to paw at the spillage.

"That's really..." Really what, gross, horrifying, sick? All valid responses, but what came out of him was, "Really cool, Billy, that's really cool." He felt like a dummy, and fear was the ventriloquist who provided voice and worked his levers.

"You should feel this, dude," his voice came in a hypnotic whisper.

"No, dude, I'm good."

"Whoa! Check this out." The trance broke, and Billy came up holding an enormous black gun.

Joey's jaw dropped open, and without conscious will, he took a step back. Billy fixed him with an icy stare. "Touch it."

Joey, mouth still slack, shook his head. "No, dude. I'm—" "I said touch it," Billy barked, and Joey's head swam.

9

Chapter 9

Thursday, May 9, 2019
Oehlerking Farm – Rural Iowa

Rodney placed the palm of his hand against the shed and felt it pulse in response. Like a spider in its web, Rodney was connected to his land, and it to him. Every root of every tree, every inch of pipe that wormed its way through the house, every nail in every board on his property, it all spoke to him, and he listened. The vibrations passed through the ground and into the rotted wooden frame of the old shed. They made their way up the frame into the rusted tin walls, and from there, into his fingertips. His web was speaking to him, and he listened. It was all telling him that the trespasser hadn't left. It told him that his prey was near, and he could feel the heavy, rapid thudding of its heart.

Rodney inhaled a deep, satisfying breath, and his own heart began to pound. Like a fist opening and closing with great force, his heart pumped. Blood rushed hot through him and eased the pain in his hands and in the fingers that gripped firmly around his hatchet. It felt good in his hand, it felt right, but it would feel better once he sunk it into the trespasser. Rodney gripped the handle tightly and moved in for the kill.

***

Ray could hear the old man's heavy breathing. It whistled in and out with each breath he took, and it was getting closer. Over his shoulder, Ray could see an open field of uneven ground and dense thickets of bull thistle. There was no way he could run through it without getting snared and cut up on the spiny weeds. His only option was to make his way out from behind the shed and bolt down the drive to the road. From there, he could run back to the neighbor's house... the one with the shotgun, and explain what was going on. *Unless that guy was in on it with this guy*, he thought, but the notion was ridiculous. *Keep it together*, man, he said to himself.

Only three years from his days of running track in college, Ray was sure he could outrun the old man, but there was no way he could outrun his car, no matter how rundown it was. He moved toward the opposite corner and could see the house a short way off. He could easily make it into the house and lock the door without the old guy catching him. But wait. *Didn't I break the lock when I pried it open?* Ray's mind moved a mile a minute as he inched away from the sound of the old man breathing and back around to the front of the shed. The front door was still standing open, and Ray decided to make a run for it. He could get inside, lock or jam something against the door, and use the guy's own phone to call the cops. Ray drew in a breath and bolted.

As he cleared the corner of the shed, a hand reached out with blinding speed and locked its fingers in his hair. Ray was yanked off his feet and fell onto his back, driving the air out of his lungs in one great burst and filling his head with stars. He lay there for a moment, struggling to draw breath. As the stars cleared, he saw the tall, lanky man standing over him, hatchet in hand and wearing what looked to Ray like a Halloween mask. The old man came down hard and fast with the hatchet.

***

The inside of the trunk was black as pitch. Sweat had soaked the duct tape, and Seneca managed to free her hands, though she couldn't see them when she held them in front of her face. She pulled the tape from around her mouth and spat out the handkerchief before ripping the tape from around her ankles. Once she was free of her bindings,

Seneca paused and listened. She could hear the wind picking up and could feel the car move in response.

Placing her hands against the interior of the trunk lid, she pushed with all she had, but it wouldn't budge. There was no way she was getting herself out of the trunk, at least not with her bare hands. Carefully, she fished around in the darkness, looking for something she might use for leverage or as a prybar. Her hand fell upon something hard.

***

Before he realized what was happening, Ray snapped his head to the side and buried the corn knife into the old man's neck. In his terror, Ray had completely forgotten he'd been holding it. Perhaps he thought he was merely throwing a punch. In his wildest dreams, Ray Borowski couldn't imagine stabbing another person with a knife. But there it was, half the blade, buried in the old man's neck. The hatchet continued its downward motion and came down hard next to Ray's face, spraying him with bits of dirt and gravel. The old man fell across Ray's legs, and he had to roll the body to the side to get up. He reached for the knife and pulled. Ray could hear and feel the blade drag across bone as it came free. The sensation made him gag, but he managed to keep from vomiting.

"Oh my God! I am so sorry, I'm so sorry! I'll

call an ambulance! You're going to be alright," Ray dropped to his knees and pressed his hands against the wound to stop the bleeding.

The old man coughed again and sprayed blood into Ray's face. It was all more than Ray could handle. The contents of his stomach sloshed, and vomit flew from his mouth and nose. It took several gut-retching contractions before he was empty.

Ray ran his forearm across his mouth. "I'm so sorry about that too," he cried.

Rodney Oehlerking lay there, his blood coming in pulsing red arcs that diminished with each spurt as it soaked the soil that his father once tended. His one good eye, the lid at half-mast, stared sightless into the darkening sky. The other, just a small, puckered hole where the eyeball should have been, looked as deep and dark as the ocean's depths to Ray. Rodney's mouth hung slack and twisted in the last expression he would ever make. Then came a final shudder, and he was gone.

A high-pitched whistle started in Ray's head and his stomach lurched again. He had just killed a man. With no food left to purge, all that came up was bile. It came up and burned his throat and sloshed like lava into his sinus cavity. Ray coughed hard to clear his throat, and then, first covering one nostril and then the other, he blew the yellow-green slime from his nose. The relief from the burning was immediate, but it was replaced by a sickly sour taste at the back of his throat. Hands on his knees, Ray breathed in and out through his mouth.

As he composed himself, Ray heard pounding from inside the trunk, and he ran to the back of the car. "Hang on, I'll get you out!" He jammed the corn knife in the gap and pried hard, breaking the latch and the blade in the process. The trunk flew open.

***

Seneca's eyes rolled wild with terror as they adjusted to the purple twilight. She could see the figure standing at the mouth of the trunk and swung the prybar as hard as she could. The first swing caught Ray along the side of the head, the second crashed hard onto his shoulder, like being knighted by a lumberjack. Ray fell to the ground, grasping his ear.

With Ray down and out, Seneca pulled herself out of the trunk and tried to run, but her legs had fallen asleep, and she struggled to stay on her feet. She didn't know where she was going. All she knew was that she wanted to put some distance between herself and that trunk. She'd only gone a few feet when she tripped and went sprawling to the ground. Seneca scrambled to her butt and moved crab-like until her back struck the shed door.

She had tripped over a man's body, and not just

any man. It was him, the man who took her. She had dropped the prybar back by the car and now found herself weaponless. Seneca drew in a breath to scream and then noticed that he wasn't moving. A huge gash in the man's neck had drawn the attention of a few buzzing flies. Disgusted and full of rage, she sprung to her feet and began kicking the body over and over.

"You motherfucker! You motherfucker!" She kicked him again and again.

"Hey! He's already dead," Ray said, holding his ripped ear to his head.

At the sound of Ray's voice, Seneca dropped to one knee and felt around for a rock or something she could use to defend herself against this new threat. Her hand fell upon Rodney's hatchet. "Stay away from me or I swear I will kill you!"

"Kill me? Are you nuts? Who do you think just got you out of that trunk?" he yelled at her as he held the side of his head and winced in pain.

Seneca, still breathing heavily, held the hatchet two-handed, the blade up next to her face. "I swear to God, I will kill you if you come near me!"

Ray wagged his head. The ringing was getting louder. He hung his jaw open and snapped his neck, hoping to make it stop, but it didn't help. Ray waved a dismissive hand at her.

"Fuck you, lady," he said and started for the

house.

Seneca watched, afraid and confused, as the man who seemed to mean her no harm — hell, who may have even saved her life — walked away. With a dead man at her feet and the wind picking up, she felt very alone. Hatchet at the ready, and with great trepidation, she followed the stranger toward the house.

***

"I don't think we should be going in there," she said as Ray climbed the porch steps.

Ray snapped his head in her direction. He hadn't realized she was following him. "I don't really give a shit what you think," he said, still holding his hand to his ear, half because of the pain and half because of the incessant ringing. If you want to stay out here and get drowned or struck by lightning, be my guest.

"Hey, I'm really sorry, I didn't—"

He glared at her. "What, didn't mean to rip my fucking ear off?"

"No, I mean, well, I thought you were—" She paused, perhaps not sure what to call her captor. "You know, the guy who grabbed me."

"Yeah, well, I'm not," he said, pushing open the door and stepping into the old farmhouse.

Inside, the house was eerily still, like it knew its master had died and it wasn't quite sure what it should be doing in his absence. A few steps in, and the house made its first sound. A loud banging came up from the basement as steam pushed through the pipes like a muffled scream. Kind of like the one Ray had heard coming from the trunk, the scream that stopped him from beating feet down that driveway and away from this godforsaken place. The scream that turned him from a bluesman to a killer. The thought made his stomach muscles contract again, and he had to steady himself. He looked at the hatchet in her hand.

"Holy shit! Is that what you hit me with? You could have fucking killed me!"

Seneca, still standing in the doorway, tucked the hatchet behind her back. "What? No! I hit you with a tire iron, or at least I think it was a tire iron."

Ray shook his head. "Thank God for small favors."

"I said I was sorry."

"No — no, you didn't. And you didn't say thank you either!"

Seneca breathed in deep, her breath hitching as a tear rolled down her cheek. "Well, I am sorry," she said.

The look on her face made Ray feel like a real shit. "No, I'm sorry. I mean, I can't imagine how scared you must have been," he said and extended a hand. "The name is Ray, Ray Borowski." *Your name is Bones, boy!* The sound surprised him and caused him to flinch. He'd almost forgotten about the voice.

Seneca jumped back and raised her hatchet at Ray's sudden movement. "Are you okay?"

"Yeah," Ray said. "I thought I heard something."

"Like what?" Seneca asked.

"So, you didn't hear anything?" Ray asked, almost pleading.

"You're scaring me."

"I'm sorry. I guess I'm just a little jumpy. Look, I'm gonna check the house, see if there's a phone."

A loud crack of thunder made them both jump, and then the rain came down. It hit the ground making a sound like someone tearing an endless sheet of paper. Ray looked out past her. "You can stay out there if you want, but you're going to get awful wet."

Seneca looked up and around the doorway and then stepped inside. Ray walked around the first floor of the house calling out a few times, but there was no response. "I don't think anyone else lives here. I think we're safe."

Ray smiled and offered his hand once again. Seneca swallowed hard and reached out with her left hand while drawing the hatchet back slightly. He took only her fingertips in his hand and released them quickly. "Nice to meet you," he said. "Even though the circumstances suck."

Seneca rubbed her forehead. "I don't even know what the hell's going on. I was waiting for a friend, and this guy grabbed me," she said, and moved her hand from her head to her neck. "The last thing I remember is him choking me. I think he brought me out here to kill me," she said and began to tremble.

"You're okay now.".

"You saved my life."

Ray leaned back against the wall. "I'm just glad I could help."

"That looks really bad."

Ray touched the mess that was his ear and winced. "I think I killed him."

"You should let me take a look at that."

"Holy shit, I really think I killed him."

"You saved my life. That animal was going to kill me, and you saved me," she said and hugged him around his middle. It was an awkward hug, almost like a child hugging a parent. "My name is Seneca, Seneca Campbell."

A flash of lightning and crash of thunder sent her flying fully into his arms. Ray could feel her trembling and held her tightly. She looked up at him, and he could see how lost she was.

He smiled reassuringly. "You're safe now."

She smiled back.

"Where're you from, Seneca?"

"I'm from Omaha, and I wish I was back home right now."

10

Chapter 10

Thursday, May 9, 2019
Tabor County, Iowa

It took some persuading, but Joey finally got Billy to leave the dead body and head home. "You go in first and distract mom, then meet me in our room," Billy said. Joey did as he was told. He considered telling his mother right then and there, but what was the best case scenario if he had? She would maybe take the gun and lock it in her glove compartment while she worked. He would still have to deal with Billy and Billy didn't need a gun or much of a reason to hurt him. No, it was better to obey his brother than try to outsmart him.

Joey talked to his mother in the living room for a moment and then met back up with his brother in their room. Joey sat on the edge of his bed and watched nervously as Billy turned the big revolver over in his hands. Even more disturbing than the gun was the grotesquely rapturous smile that had formed on Billy's face. Joey knew that smile and it sent a chill up his spine. It was the same smile Joey had seen two years ago, when Billy broke his arm, and the smile he had first seen when Billy was only seven years old. The summer that their neighbor's cat disappeared. The same summer he'd learned not to tattle on his big brother.

Their neighbors, the Griffins, had a fat, orange tabby named Gilligan. Everyone in the neighborhood hated that cat because the Griffins would let Gilligan roam free and shit anywhere it wanted. Gilligan would shit in sandboxes, flower gardens, mulch piles, and the Griffins would never clean up after him. When Billy was seven, he caught Gilligan in their backyard, getting ready to drop a deuce in the little sandbox the previous owners had left when they moved. Billy snatched Gilligan up and told Joey that he was going to toss it over the fence at the back of their yard. He told Joey to wait for him and not to follow.

Joey did as he was told. He watched his big brother carry the cat to the back fence, but then, instead of tossing it over like he said, Billy took the cat behind the shed. Joey heard hissing and wild mewing and then nothing. It was a full ten minutes before Billy emerged from behind the shed. Only there was something different about his big brother. Billy's eyes were clouded over, and his face was contorted into that horrible smile.

Joey was frozen but managed to squeak out, "You okay, Billy?"

But Billy walked right by him. It was like he didn't even notice him. He walked straight past him and into the house, letting the screen door slam behind him, which always pissed their dad off. But the bang was like a starter's pistol that freed Joey from the blocks. He sprinted to the shed and found Gilligan lying in the dirt with his neck twisted fully around so that even as it was laying prone, its dead sightless eyes stared up at him.

That night at supper, Joey couldn't eat. His mother asked him what was wrong, but he wouldn't answer. She threatened to send him to bed without supper if he didn't answer her, but that was fine with Joey. Then their father chimed in. He told Joey that if he didn't answer his mother, he would beat his ass so hard that he wouldn't be able to sit down for a week. Reluctantly, Joey told them about Gilligan. Billy said he was lying, and they all walked out to the shed. The cat's body was gone. Maybe Billy got rid of it, or perhaps some other animal had carried it off. Joey didn't know, but he got spanked and grounded for a week. But that wasn't what taught him not to squeal on his brother. That night as the family slept, Joey woke to the feeling of something cold and hard against his neck. He opened his eyes to see Billy standing over him with a butcher's knife pressed to his throat. Billy held a finger to his lips. "Shh, if you say a word, I'll slit your throat."

Billy led him out to the shed and pushed the tip of the knife into his stomach, not so hard as to penetrate, but hard enough so that he could feel the tip through his pajama shirt. "You ever rat on me again, and I promise, you'll get worse than that fuckin' cat got."

Billy didn't ask him if he understood. He didn't say another word, just turned and walked back toward the house. In the days that followed, Billy acted as if nothing had happened. The neighbors stopped finding cat shit in their sandboxes, flower gardens, and mulch piles, and that was the end of that. Then other peoples' pets began disappearing. The Fensters' rabbit, even the Mulcahys' dog. Signs went up all over the neighborhood, but Chestnut was never found. Joey knew what happened, but he never said a word. And now that smile was back, and Joey had a gun.

"Hurry up, boys. I have to leave for work," Joanna called from the kitchen.

His mother's voice snapped him back from the

memory and Joey could feel his palms begin to sweat.. Thinking fast, he said, "I'm really sick, Mom."

Billy just stared at the gun and smiled his terrible smile. Joey could feel the panic setting in. Their mom would be leaving for work in a few minutes, and he couldn't imagine what was going on inside that head with the terrible smile pasted to it.

"What's wrong with you?" Joanna asked.

"I puked before," Joey said.

"Maybe I should stay home," she said.

The sound of the conversation seemed to draw Billy's attention. "What the fuck is your problem, Joey?" he whispered harshly.

"I don't know, Billy. I think I'm sick."

"Bullshit, you were fine all day."

"Well, I'm not now," he fired back.

"Keep your voice down," Billy snarled.

"Billy, you shouldn't have taken that." The utterance flew from his mouth as uncontrolled as the vomit had been.

Billy glared at him, but the words were out, and there was no way to un-ring that bell. Still, he had to try. "Maybe we can put it back."

"Maybe," Billy spun and pointed the gun at Joey's head, "you should shut your fucking mouth."

Billy took a step toward Joey, then another and another until Joey was backed against their bedroom wall. Joey turned his face away from the gun, and Billy put the barrel to the side of his head. He pushed hard against his little brother's temple.

"I'm sorry, Billy," Joey winced. "I just don't want to see you get in trouble."

Billy eased up on the pressure and lowered the gun. "Wow, thanks, Joey," he said, offering a warm smile.

Joey breathed a sigh of relief and smiled sickly back at his brother.

Then Billy's smile turned into a sneer. "Thanks a shit-load, Joey."

He grabbed his brother by the hair on the top of his head and pinned it against the wall. Then he pressed the barrel to Joey's lips and pushed hard enough to split the skin. Joey could taste the blood and opened his mouth against the pain. Billy slid the barrel in deep enough to cause him to gag.

"Joey, are you throwing up again?" Joanna called from the other side of the closed door.

"He's okay, Mom." Billy smiled sweetly as the words came out, but the fire was still in his eyes. Then he turned his full attention back on Joey and continued through gritted teeth. "If you're think-ing about telling Mom—" Billy's eyes narrowed like he was struggling to read his little brother's mind "—or the cops... so help me, if you tell the cops, you'll be dead before I go to jail, I promise you."

Joey felt the warm sensation of piss running down his leg.

"What are you two doing? I said get cleaned up and get your asses out here!"

"Be right out, Mom. I'm just helping Joey."

Billy pulled the gun barrel out of Joey's mouth. The front sight hooked the skin on his upper lip and ripped the cut open even more.

"If I have to open this door—"

"Coming, Mom!" Billy stashed the gun under his pillow. "Go change your pants," he sneered and plowed through the door. "I was just making sure Joey was okay. He did something to his mouth. I think he bit his lip or something."

"Joey, come out here, now!"

Joey came out of the room; he was white as a sheet. Joanna placed her hand on his forehead. "You don't feel warm, but you look flushed," she said. She stood there with her hands on her hips and looking a bit lost. "I don't know, we really can't afford for me to miss my shift," she said, glancing at the pile of bills on the battered old kitchen table. "But I don't want to leave you if you're really sick."

Joey forced his face to droop even further, but it was difficult because her words were like an elixir that made his terror begin to fade. Then Billy spoke.

"I'll be with him, Mom, and I promise to call if

he doesn't start feeling better."

"I don't know," she said, chewing her lower lip. "You got the number?"

Billy pointed to a Prickly Pete's Bar and Grill magnet on the freezer door of their avocado green fridge. The magnet featured a caricature of Pete and his trademark stubble, shoving a terrified-looking cartoon catfish into a deep fryer. "Right here, Mom."

Joanna smiled and tousled both of their hair. "You really are two good boys," she said with a mother's smile. Then the smile faded to anger, "Not like your piece-of-shit father." And then to a look of worry. "You sure you boys will be okay?"

Joey wanted to scream. He wanted to shout in his mother's face. *No, no, I'm not going to be okay, you fucking idiot! Your other son is a lunatic, and he's going to murder me! Maybe not tonight, but it's gonna happen! Sure as God made little green apples, lady, he's going to kill me!* But Joey said nothing. Instead, he smiled sickly and tried to communicate his feelings with his eyes, but she missed his signals. *Fuck!* She could be so dense when she wanted to be.

"We'll be fine, Mom," Billy said.

Joanna Parks smiled lovingly. "I'm leaving my phone on the charger, the battery's running low. I'll be home around 12:30. No going out, ya hear? Tomorrow is a school day."

"Yes, Mom," Billy said.

Joey watched as his brother played their mother like a fiddle. He smiled at her and blinked his eyes, and she melted like butter. *Un-fucking-believable*, he thought. His brother was the absolute worst person he knew, even worse than the no-good piece of shit, but somehow he never got in trouble. It was like their mother wanted to believe him so badly that she never smelled the bullshit, even when he was waving a big-ole plateful right under her nose. Billy watched his mother get in the car and offered a bull-shitty wave as she drove away. Then he turned toward Joey.

"She's gone. Come on, we're going back out there."

"But Billy, that's over an hour walk, man. I'm tired."

"Don't be such a pussy!"

"But Mom said—"

"I know what Mom said." Billy pulled the gun out from under his pillow. "Now *I'm* saying, we're going back out there. So, let's go, or the first bullet is going to be for you. You, got it?"

"Yes, I got it."

Joey looked around their shitty little house, realizing that it might be the last time he would ever see it. The shitty TV on the shitty TV stand, the shitty recliner with the broken armrest that his mom bought at a garage sale, the shitty rust-colored shag carpet that covered the whole place like a fuzzy scab. It was all shitty, but it was his home. Joey walked out of the house like a man stepping out of his prison cell to walk his last mile.

He was used to the feeling of impending doom. It came with the territory when you were an under-sized boy of thirteen, and even more so when you had a brother like Billy. But this was different. He'd always done his best to appease his brother. To keep him happy. Kind of the way his mother handled his father, the no-good-piece-of-shit. But he could see the black beginning to cloud the whites of Billy's eyes, and he had learned that once the black took over, there was just no getting around what was coming.

As they walked, Joey had replayed the broken elbow incident over and over in his head, hoping to find some way to escape whatever was coming. Was there something he could have done two summers ago? Something he might have done to deescalate the situation? He could have fought back, but no, that was just plain stupid. Billy would have probably killed him. His mom had tried that once with the no-good-piece-of-shit, and that landed her in the emergency room. He could have run, but Will Munger had his bike there that day. Billy would have shoved Will off the bike, rode after him, and caught him. That would have probably ended with two broken arms and a fat lip.

"Let's go, Joey, or so help me," Billy said, and for good measure, he placed his hand on the pistol butt that stuck out of the front of his jeans.

Yes, it was different this time, and Joey knew it. He hurried out the door after his brother. He followed close enough behind Billy so that Billy knew he was following, but far enough that he could turn and run if he had to.

"Come on, Joey. Keep up."

"I'm trying," he said, doing his best to sound out of breath.

"Well, try harder! It's already too dark to see where we're going, and I don't want to forget where the body was."

Billy picked up the pace, tugging constantly at his belt to keep his pants from being dragged down by the weight of the gun. They had come upon the body by accident — or maybe accident wasn't the right word. It seemed to Joey that his brother had a sort of sixth sense when it came to finding bad things. Like he had some kind of terrible magnet in him that threw his internal compasses, both moral and directional, horribly out of whack.

Earlier in the day, Billy forced him to take a shortcut through a part of the woods that no kids — at least not the ones they hung out with — ever went into. Not since the summer Richie Barrett went missing for three days. A hunter and his dog found Richie's body. It had been mutilated, torn apart. Some people, their mother included, said that it must have been a mountain lion, but the good-for-nothing-piece-of-shit said that it couldn't have been a mountain lion. He said it was probably an escaped mental patient from one of the state mental hospitals, either the one in Des Moines or the one in Independence. It didn't matter that no escapes had been reported. The good-for-nothing-piece-of-shit said escapes happened all the time and that the newspapers never reported them because they didn't want the people to panic. Joanna, their mother, said he was full of shit, but to his credit, the P.O.S. offered an explanation rather than a beating. One that Joey found totally reasonable.

"First of all, you dumb bitch," his father said, "mountain lions don't come this deep into the state. And B, if it was a mountain lion that done that kid that way, then why is Iowa DNR kicking around the idea of upping the limit from two to three tags for deer this year? A mountain lion is a fuckin' super-predator. Damn thing kills at least a deer a week, and when a super-predator shows up, deer split. So, tell me, Einstein, why is the deer population explodin' if there's a mountain lion out there? That wasn't no mountain lion. That was

the super-est predator of 'em all, that was a man."
Joey remembered the P.O.S. squinting and looking
off into the distance when he said it, like an actor
delivering the clincher in an action movie. Piece of
shit or no piece of shit, their dad had a point. But
that had been years ago, there was no way that guy
could still be around. Still, something killed the guy
they found earlier.

And sure as shit, Billy's fucked-up compass led
them right to the body. And not just any body, but
the body of a dead cop. They walked the shortcut
but Joey refused to cross the footbridge so they took
the longer route around, and that was where they
found it. The guy's face was chopped up pretty
good, and his stomach was cut wide open, and some
of his guts had spilled out. As soon as he saw it, Joey
knew the nightmares were going to be brutal. But
then Billy decided to kick things up a notch. Billy
said that he wanted to know what a dead body felt
like. He placed his hand on the body. He said it felt
warm but rubbery. That was gross, but Joey could
have written that off as curiosity. Then Billy began
pulling on the cop's intestines. He was like some
evil magician doing a version of the handkerchief
trick straight out of a magic show from hell. Billy
stretched the intestines out as far as they would go
and then looped them in a circle around the dead
body.

"That oughta creep out anybody who comes by," Billy said, wiping his hands on the officer's pants before stealing his gun.

Joey wasn't sure he would ever forget the sight of that body, and now, here he was, venturing back into the forbidden woods because Billy said he had to. They'd only gone about fifty yards in when a rustling noise and a bouncing beam from a flashlight up ahead made them stop.

"Billy, we should go back home," he said. "What if the guy who killed the cop came back? What if he's the same guy that did that stuff to Richie?"

Billy stroked his chin. "You think so? You think it's the killer? They always return to the scene of the crime, right?" Billy's eyes widened. "If it is, it's probably not even against the law to kill him, right?"

Billy's words were an epiphany to Joey. Maybe that could be the best thing that could happen. Billy could scratch his itch, and Joey wouldn't have to suffer for it. "I bet you're right, Billy. I bet you would be a hero!"

Joey had no idea how the law would look at such a thing. He was a boy of thirteen; what the hell did he know about anything? But he figured it would beat the alternative. Then he had another thought. What if it were the cops up ahead? If Billy jumped out at a cop while holding a gun, the cop would definitely blow him away. If Billy got lucky and shot the cop, then Billy would go to juvi. Try as he might, Joey couldn't see a downside.

"Get him, Billy," he urged.

Billy drew the gun from his waistband and signaled for Joey to follow. Joey followed but stayed a few feet back, back and off to the side. He didn't want to end up as collateral damage if there was an exchange of gunfire. As they neared the source of the light, the beam turned quickly in their direction and held there. Joey sucked in a deep gulp of air and froze. As he stood there holding his breath, he could feel his heart pounding, first in his chest and then in his throat. His lungs began to burn, and there was no way he could let it back out quietly. He tried to force a little air in through his nose, but his lungs were completely full, and it made him feel like he wanted to cough. He began to feel dizzy, and then he heard the oddest sound. Not odd in and of itself, but odd for the circumstances. It was a cell phone, and it was ringing.

The beam from the light darted in the direction of the ringing phone, and Joey blew the stale air out of his lungs and dove for the ground. In the still, dark woods, there was something almost sacrilegious in the sound, and Joey wished someone would make it stop. But the damned thing just kept ringing. Joey kept his face close to the ground and worked to slow his breathing. He clamped his hands over his ears, but he could still hear the phone. Joey pressed his eyes shut and tried to ignore it, and it stopped, but now something else was pushing its way into his head.

It was the smell. The wind had shifted, and the stench of the dead deputy was hitting him again. It was the worst smelling thing he'd ever encountered, and that included the dead mouse in their bedroom wall. The one their landlord, Mr. Tedeschi, took almost a month to get rid of. Joey's mind was ripped from the memory by a single gunshot and then nothing.

Joey lay prone in the grass, his ears ringing. The shot seemed impossibly loud, and as he got to his feet, everything seemed muffled, like someone had stuffed his ears full of cotton. Joey worked his jaw and popped his fingers in and out of his ears, trying to clear them. Slowly his hearing returned, and he began walking in the direction of the gunshot. The flashlight lay on the ground, throwing its cold white beam across the body that gurgled and clutched at its neck as blood rushed between its fingers. Joey tried, but he couldn't look away. He just dropped to the ground and stared.

11

Chapter 11

Thursday, May 9, 2019
Oehlerking Farm – Rural Iowa

Seneca pushed gently out of Ray's arms, and he hated to let her go. It wasn't the feel of her chest heaving against his or even the smell of her hair. It just felt good to hold her, to feel a human connection in such an inhumane environment. And if nothing else, it took his mind off his ruined ear, but Ray let her slip from his arms. Outside, lightning flashed behind the dirt-caked windows, and thunder shook the house.

"It sounds like it's getting worse out there," Ray said.

"You really should let me look at that," Seneca said, reaching toward the bloody flap that was his ear.

Ray jerked his head back instinctively. "No offense, but I think I need a doctor."

"Well, I don't see one around, do you? Besides, I'm studying to be a P.A."

"Like an announcer?"

"What?" Confusion clouded her face, and Ray read it as if she were wondering if he was an idiot.

"No, a physician's assistant. We're like doctors, but we don't get paid as well." She offered a soft smile.

Reluctantly, Ray removed his hand from his ear and leaned toward her. The bare bulb that hung from the ceiling flickered and then brightened.

Seneca glanced up. "Well, that's better," she said, and then examined the ear. "You're going to need a couple of stitches, and we are going to need to sterilize the wound. Let me see what I can find to fix that up."

"Don't go too far. I mean, I think he lived alone, but we can't be sure," he said, marveling at her composure.

"I won't. Sit down at the table," she called from the doorway that Ray presumed was the bathroom.

She returned carrying a little metal box. "I found this. I think it's the best we're going to do. But there's no peroxide or rubbing alcohol."

Rodney's blood was still on the needle, and Seneca handled it carefully. "I'm going to need to sterilize this somehow. And we're going to have to clean your wound before I stitch it up, otherwise it's going to get infected."

Seneca looked around the kitchen, found a pot, and filled it from the faucet. The pipes rattled and hissed and then spat rust-colored water into the sink.

"Holy crap," Ray said. "You can't be serious."

"Relax," she said. "Give it a minute."

After clearing its throat, the faucet poured clear water into the sink. Seneca studied it. "It looks clean, but we can't risk an infection." She filled the pot and set it on the stove.

Seneca turned the knob, but the stove didn't light. "Figures," she rolled her eyes. "My grandmother had a stove like this. My grandparents lived in an old farmhouse." She began rummaging through drawers close by. "She kept a box of matches... here we go."

Seneca pulled a box of stick matches out of a drawer. She took two of the matches out of the box, broke the tips off, and set them aside. The third match was used to light the pilot. While she waited for the water to boil, she looked through the cabinets until she found some salt. She found a spoon in a drawer and used it to skim the foam off the top of the water and then dumped all the salt from the shaker into the pot. She looked around the kitchen for a dish towel, but the only thing she found was a moldy-smelling rag.

"Close your eyes," she said.

"Why, what for? What are you going to do?" Ray asked nervously.

"Relax, I need my t-shirt. Yours is filthy. Now close your eyes."

Ray closed his eyes for a second and then raised his eyelids to slits so that he could see. He watched as Seneca unzipped her hoodie and took it off. She pulled her t-shirt over her head. Whoever said that more than a handful was a waste was out of their freaking mind. *She owes you, boy. You saved her life.* The voice didn't startle him this time. He shook his head to clear it, sending a spike of pain through his ear. Seneca pinned her shirt between her knees and then zipped the sweatshirt back up.

"Okay, you can open your eyes," she said.

Seneca tore the shirt into ragged strips and dipped one of the strips into the saline solution and gently dabbed his ear. Ray winced. "Serves you right. I saw you peeking." Ray blushed.

With the wound cleaned, Seneca used the two broken matches as makeshift tweezers and heated the needle over the burner until it was glowing. When it cooled, she removed the char with the rag and threaded the needle.

"This is going to hurt."

Ray guessed that she was around his age. Ray would be twenty-five in September. He'd done his stint in college, but unlike Seneca, that was the end of his formal education. Seneca, on the other hand, chose a field of service, and now here she was, fresh out of a kidnapper's trunk, applying her craft. Ray marveled at her. He marveled at the ferocity she had shown when she clocked him with the tire iron and the tenderness she was showing now. He marveled at the skill of her hands and the softness in her eyes.

"I can't imagine what you must be going through."

"It's been quite a day," she said, still focused on her work.

"After this storm rolls through," lightning flashed and thunder peeled as if to make his point, "we'll find that guy's keys and get the hell out of here."

"Sounds good to me," she said and snapped the thread. "There, all done. That wasn't so bad, was it?"

Ray raised his hand toward his ear, but Seneca grabbed him by the wrist. "You're going to have to leave it alone."

Outside, the storm seemed to be reaching a fevered pitch. The walls of the house began to creak and moan against the wind. As if sensing that Seneca was done, the lights flickered again and dimmed back to a normal brightness. Ray shot to his feet.

"Shit!"

"What?"

"My guitar! It's out there."

Ray ran to the door and pulled it open. He shielded his ear from the rain as best he could and took the first blast of cold rain in the face. Pulling his hand from his forehead to his chin like a squeegee, Ray flew behind the car and grabbed his belongings. Halfway back to the house, he froze in his tracks.

"Seneca!"

"Yeah?" she called from the porch.

Ray yelled something, but a thunder crash covered his response.

"What?"

Ray suddenly got the feeling that something was watching him, and he bolted for the house. He took the stairs in a single bound, pulled her inside, and slammed the door shut. He dropped his gear, the guitar's strings humming flatly in its case, and he fumbled for the deadbolt.

"Ray, you're scaring me. What's wrong?"

"His body... it's — it's gone."

Seneca clenched her jaw and balled up her fists. He could see that her body was ready to fight, but her eyes said something different. Her eyes told a tale of pain and fear and exhaustion, and Ray admired the shit out of her. They walked back into the kitchen.

"We have to find him and finish him," she said as she picked up the hatchet from the table.

"I think we should look for a phone and call the police."

Out of habit, Seneca reached for her pocket, but her phone was gone. "My cell phone," she patted her front and back pants pockets, "I must have lost it. Do you have one?"

"It's a long story."

Ray had a cell phone, but he left it on his night-stand when he left home. He wanted to make it to Chicago on his wits and his talent. A cell phone would have been a distraction, and besides, he figured it would be kind of cool for his fans that followed him on social media to wonder what happened to him.

"Did you have it in the trunk?"

"I don't know, maybe."

"Okay, let's make sure this place is secure and see if there's a landline. If there is, we can call for help. If not, we can go out and check the trunk. How does that sound?"

Seneca gripped the hatchet tighter, swallowed hard and nodded.

"You want me to take that?" Ray asked.

Seneca hugged the weapon to her body, and Ray held his hands up in a gesture that communicated that he understood her apprehensiveness. He opened one of the kitchen drawers and found a single butter knife, fork, and spoon. "Well, I guess that answers our question about whether he lived alone or not."

Ray grabbed the pot off the stove and dumped the water in the sink. He felt the weight of the thing in his hand. "Shit, they don't make 'em like this anymore," he said and swung it a few times, imagining making contact with the crazy fucker's head.

Seneca nodded, wide-eyed, and they began their search. There was a pantry off the kitchen, so they decided to start there. There was no door, just hinges that looked to have been painted over long ago. Instead of being filled with dry goods or things one might use in the kitchen, the floor and shelves were littered with coffee cans, both empty and full.

Satisfied that nothing in the pantry posed a risk, they turned to the parlor. A full-sized bed sat near the center of the room against the east wall. There was a nightstand to the left of the lumpy, piss-stained mattress and a small dresser to the right near the entrance to the room, but that was it. As spartan a decorating style as he'd ever seen.

"I think we're okay down here." No sooner had

Ray spoken than they heard a loud thud from above.

Ray firmed up his grip on the pot handle and crossed the room. A steep, narrow staircase in the kitchen led to the second floor of the desolate farmhouse. The sun had fully set, and except for the occasional flash of lightning, the second floor sat in darkness. Ray set his foot on the first step. The loud creak made Seneca jump worse than the noise from upstairs.

"Why do we even need to go up there?" she asked in a whisper.

Living on the road, even for such a short time, Ray had begun to develop street smarts. Without really realizing it, Ray had analyzed their situation. He answered, doing his best not to sound like he was talking down to her.

"It doesn't look like there's a landline in this place, so calling for help is out of the question."

"What about my cell?"

"If it's in the trunk, I can pretty much guarantee the rain trashed it. The trunk was wide open when I went out there. It's probably a bathtub by now."

Seneca's face fell.

"Look, we're probably going to have to spend the night here."

"What? Hell no!"

"Listen to me," Ray said, wincing as the ringing in his ear started again.

"What's wrong? Is it your ear?"

"What? No, it's fine," he said, shaking it off. "Look, if that guy is out there, we won't make it to the end of the driveway. He's probably a hunter, and so far, I haven't seen any guns in the house, which means he probably had his rifle in the car. I say we barricade the door to make sure he can't get in, check the second floor and sit tight for the night."

Seneca wrapped her arms around herself, still clutching tightly to the hatchet. Ray understood her apprehension. Hell, he was apprehensive about scaling the stairs up into the pitch black of the second floor armed with only a pot, but, in his opinion, they didn't have much choice. After jamming one of the kitchen chairs under the doorknob as a brace, they walked over to the stairs.

"I'll go up by myself if you want. If something happens to me, you can still run."

Seneca didn't speak.

"When you hit the end of the driveway, go right. There's a house about five miles up the road. The guy answered the door with a shotgun, but he didn't shoot. Tell him what's going on."

Seneca began shaking her head.

"I don't know if he has a phone, but he can keep a lot of shit at bay with that side-by-side."

"No," she finally said. "I'm not leaving you. If

you're going up, then I'm going up with you."

"You're sure you can swing that thing at a person if it comes to it?"

She tilted her head, and again, Ray caught her meaning. "Right," he said and raised a hand to his ear.

Step by creaking step, they went up into the darkness. Halfway up, Ray remembered his Zippo and fished it out of his pocket. He flipped the top open with a ping and thumbed the flint wheel. The lighter bathed the landing in a warm orange glow that would have been comforting if not for the circumstances. Ray found a button switch on the wall and pushed it. The lights overhead — just two bare bulbs that hung from the ceiling, just like in the kitchen, flickered and went out.

"Who the fuck did the electric in this place?" Ray said as he pushed the buttons off and on.

Seneca, who had wrapped her free hand around his middle and halted, "We shouldn't be up here, Ray. This feels wrong."

He could feel it too, but he wondered if they were feeling the same thing. He could feel it in his bones. And he didn't mean that as an idiom. Ray could literally *feel* it. His knuckles ached, and his hands stiffened.

"We'll do a quick check and get back downstairs," he said.

Ray tucked the pot under his arm and turned the knob on the door to the first room. A sewing machine and a lamp sat below a window. Ray slid his hand up the wall, his fingers growing stiffer by the minute. He found another button switch and thumbed the button. There was a click, but no light.

"Shit!"

Ray pulled the pot from under his arm and held the Zippo high in the air. They moved through the room slowly. A chair, a closet stuffed with bolts of white fabric, and a creepy torso were all the first room had to offer. The second room was occupied by a huge four-poster bed that took up most of the floor space. Ray tried to drop to one knee, but Seneca grabbed his wrist.

"What are you doing?" Seneca asked.

"Well, I gotta check under the bed, don't I?"

"Nothing good comes from looking under beds," she said.

He gave her a cockeyed stare, and Seneca seemed to take his point, but that didn't mean she liked the idea. Seneca followed him down to the floor. Ray set his pot down and lifted the dust-ruffle. It had done its job. A cloud of dust fell and scattered into the air, causing Ray to sneeze violently and snap the Zippo shut. With the lighter out, they sat in the darkness staring into the black beneath the bed.

"Ray," she gripped his forearm.

As he stared into the void, his thumb resting solidly on the flint-wheel, Ray thought of Schrödinger's Cat. Until he spun the wheel, striking the flint and bringing the Zippo to life, there existed two truths. There was both something and nothing under the bed, and only by lighting the Zippo would he eliminate one of the truths.

Seneca tightened her grip. "Ray..."

He braced himself and dragged his thumb across the wheel. The dust particles in the air ignited in a burst of orange that shrunk his pupils like the flash of a camera, and for a moment, all he saw was the fuzzy glow of the Zippo's flame dancing in front of him. He pressed his eyes shut, half in an attempt to clear his vision and half against the thing he could sense inches from his face. He could smell something sour and feel cold air puffing, like breath passing across his face. He could hear a clicking, like a dog's nails across a wooden floor, and a rattling rasp of an inhale before each puff. Ray braced himself and forced his eyes open. Slowly his vision came into focus, and he found himself staring at the mummified remains of a cat.

Ray exhaled in relief. "There's your answer, Schrödinger."

"Ray, I heard that thing breathing."

"It's a dead cat, Seneca. By the looks of it, it hasn't drawn a breath in ten years."

"I don't like this place."

"Neither do I, but we can't let our imaginations get the better of us."

They got up and made their way to the third room. This room, the sparsest of all, seemed to be a child's bedroom, though it was missing a bed. Other than a couple of sloppy crayon drawings and a faded sports pennant that someone had tacked to the door, there was absolutely nothing to see in the third room.

Standing before the final room, Ray could see light spilling from the gap between the bottom of the door and the floor. He was fairly certain that the room had been dark only a moment ago, but he knew that he couldn't trust his memory — or the wires in the walls. So far, they'd been lucky. Every room they had checked was empty, but how long would their luck hold out?

"If there's someone else in this house, they are in this room," he said, sweeping his arm back, moving Seneca away from the door before joining her out of the doorway. He decided that he was going to knock on the final door and didn't want to catch the blast from some trigger-happy redneck on the other side of the door.

He gave two good raps on the door. "Hello?" And braced for the sound of the blast, but it didn't come. "Hello?" He knocked again. "My name is Ray Borowski. I'm a musician, and my friend here, she's a doctor."

"I'm actually studying to be a P.A.," Seneca of-fered.

Ray rolled his eyes. "Look, we're not going to hurt you. We just want to use your phone."

Still, there was no answer from inside. "I'm going to open the door. Please don't shoot!" Ray reached for the knob and froze when he saw a shadow pass through the light under the door. Seneca must have seen it, too, because she clung so tightly to Ray that he couldn't draw a deep breath.

"You're gonna break my ribs."

"I'm sorry," she whispered. "Someone's in there!"

"No shit!"

"Let's get out of here," she insisted. "I'll take my chances running for it."

Ray could feel the rise and fall of her chest as she pressed against his back. He thought that he could even feel her heart pounding but then thought that it might have been his own heart that he was feeling. They had both been through a hell of a lot, and odds were, the fucker he thought he'd killed was waiting on the other side of the door. Ray had had enough.

"Listen, asshole! You kidnapped this girl, and we are calling the police, so you better give yourself up! You hear me, asshole?" Ray slammed the pot against the door several times and then grabbed the knob and turned.

The door flew open. Ray paused, waiting for the shot, and then rushed into the room, waving the pot over his head like some lunatic going into battle. Seneca followed with her hatchet at the ready, and then they both stopped. A small table sat against the far wall just below a window, like the sewing machine in the other room. On the table, a bare-bulbed lamp flickered weakly, but that was it.

"There's no one here, Ray," she said.

"I can see that," he said, scanning the room. "What is this guy's deal with lampshades?"

"I don't know, but can we please go back down-stairs?"

They made their way down, both breathing a little easier, while something twirled lazily in the darkest corner on the second floor and then seeped through the wall, slipping out into the storm.

12

Chapter 12

Thursday, May 9, 2019, 10:25 PM
Tabor County, Iowa

T ammy Cooper walked into the Tabor County Dispatch Center ready to start her shift. She greeted the room with a cheerful hello, but no one responded. She felt a little slighted, but she was only one shift away from her first Friday off in a decade, and she wasn't about to let these bitches get her down. Tammy had worked for the county for nearly ten years and finally she got Fridays and Saturdays off, so she would get through whatever bullshit this shift brought and spend Friday night forgetting all about it.

Shrugging off the snub, Tammy walked into the break room and reached for the coffee pot. It was cold as ice which meant it had been sitting there for at least an hour and no one thought to make another pot. She grabbed the filter basket, walked over to the garbage can and slammed it good and hard against the side, making sure everyone could hear.

"Can't anyone make a pot of coffee?"

There was no response from the comm center. She tossed her dinner into the fridge, walked out to her dispatch terminal and plugged in just as Nicole and Mandi, her shiftmates, entered the room. Slowly, Tammy began to notice the worried looks on the other dispatchers' faces.

"Evening ladies," Nicole said, addressing the group. No one responded.

"What's up their asses?" Mandi asked, loud enough for all to hear.

"No idea," stammered Tammy, who was starting to feel a little worried herself.

Tina, the dispatch center's director, stepped over to Tammy's terminal and motioned for Nicole and Mandi to join them. They stowed their lunches in the fridge and made their way over.

"It's Deputy Lawson," Tina said. "He hasn't answered his status checks since he went 10-08 after his dinner break at 1700 hours."

Tammy looked at the big clock that hung on the wall — the same clock she had been staring at as it ticked off the seconds of her life for the past ten years. It was a quarter to eleven. That meant it had been almost six hours since anyone had heard from Lawson, and that was unusual. Lawson was an FNG, a fucking new guy, and like all FNGs, he was good for a couple of stops an hour at the very least.

"They do that shit all the time," Nicole said. "They turn their fucking portables down to listen to a game or something on the car stereo and forget to turn them back up."

"Nic's right," Mandi agreed. "Johansen went a whole shift without turning on his radio."

"Yeah, but Lawson's an FNG. He can't go half an hour without making a stop," Beth said. Beth Cruz had taken Lawson's 10-08, available for service, call when he cleared from his dinner break and called out his first status check at 1800 hours. Lawson never responded.

Tammy knew Nicole was right, but so was Beth. "Have we toned him?" The tension in the room spread like a virus.

"About a hundred times," Beth answered.

"Maybe we can tone him again, now that it's shift change?" Tammy suggested.

Tina gave her the go-ahead nod and Tammy hit the tone button. It emitted a high-pitched droning sound that sent a shiver down the spines of even veteran officers. The sound meant bad news was coming. Fatal crashes, bank robberies, active shooters, but by now, every officer in Tabor County knew what the tone was for.

"Deputy Lawson, status check, Deputy Robert Lawson, what is your status?" Tammy said and unkeyed her mic.

Again, there was no response.

"Maybe his portable died?" Mandi said, doing her best to sound hopeful.

"He'd still hear his in-car-radio," Tina said.

"What about pinging his car? Have we tried that?" Tammy asked.

The dispatch center fell dead silent.

"Every hour on the hour," Tina said.

Worry clouded Beth's face. "It's like his cruiser just disappeared."

"Beth, would you try pinging it again?" Tina asked.

They all sat silently waiting for the response. Sitting and worrying was nothing new to dispatchers. All across the country dispatchers would send their officers into dangerous situations and then be forced to wait until the officers cleared to know that their guys were okay. But there had been no call for service and Deputy Lawson hadn't initiated a traffic stop. He simply had not answered his status check for over six hours.

"Does anyone have his cell number?" Tina asked.

They all had it, and they had all tried calling

him on his cell. "I've tried it over and over," Beth answered. "I'm really worried."

Tabor County was over seven hundred square miles of land and fifteen hundred miles of roads, not counting the myriad nameless back roads not maintained by the Tabor County Department of Roads or the various municipal entities. Finding one missing car in that seemingly endless sea of black ribbon was daunting to say the least. And with no ping response, it would take nothing short of dumb luck or a miracle to find him.

Tina grabbed a terminal and announced, "All Tabor County Units, emergency traffic only, repeat, emergency traffic only, on channel one. Switch to channel three and stand by for a roll call." Then, addressing Nicole, she said, "Would you man channel three tonight?

Nicole sighed, but Tammy wouldn't have minded the assignment. It would have taken her mind off of the missing deputy. The call center was quiet for the next half hour. At 11:35 PM, the jangle of the ringing phone shot through the dispatchers like a bolt of electricity. Nicole and Mandi tightened ranks around Tammy's console.

"9-1-1, what's your emergency?" She was hoping to hear Lawson's voice.

"It's my boys, I just got home from work and they're not here."

"I understand, what's your name?" Tammy asked and shook her head to let the center know that it wasn't the call they'd been hoping for.

"Parks, Joanna Parks. I live at 5N751 Burns Court."

"And how old are your sons?"

"Joey is thirteen and Billy is fifteen. Tomorrow is a school day and they know they're not allowed out past ten on school nights."

"Yes ma'am. Do either of the boys have any medical conditions?"

"No! Why are you wasting time with this? I need a cop out here now!"

"My partner has already dispatched an officer. If you can just stay with me a little longer."

"I'm sorry," Joanna said. "It's just so hard raising teenage boys on your own."

Tammy could hear the stress in her caller's voice. "I can only imagine," she said, doing her best to sound empathetic. "Can you tell me what they were wearing when you last saw them?"

"Jeans, t-shirts, I don't know, the shit teenage boys wear. Are you sure they're coming? I'm in unincorporated Tabor County."

"Yes ma'am. The deputy is on his way. Now can you—"

"Son of a bitch! Where in the hell have you been?" Across the center, Tammy heard Deputy Rollins call out 10-60 in the area.

"Ma'am?"

"Yeah, I'm sorry to bother you, they just walked in the door."

"Yes ma'am, the deputy has just advised that he's in the area. He should be pulling up any minute. He's going to want to talk to you now, so we'll disconnect."

"Okay, and again, I am so sorry to trouble you."

***

Joanna ended the call and set her cell phone back on the counter. Billy walked in first and bolted straight for their bedroom. Joey followed a little behind and looked white as a sheet. Joanna wanted to scream at him but stopped herself. There was something wrong with her baby boy. She put her palm to his forehead. He felt clammy.

"Joey, what's wrong?"

Joey just stared dumbly at her.

"Are you on drugs? Joey, what's wrong?"

Her hands began to shake; she'd never seen him like that before. He looked hollow, like someone or something had just scooped out everything that made him her special little guy.

"Joey, baby, you're scaring mommy. Please tell me what's wrong."

As she knelt holding her son, there came a hard rap at the door. "Tabor County Sheriff's Depart-

147

ment," the voice called out.

Joey's eyes widened and his jaw dropped open.

Billy stepped from the bedroom door behind Joey and Joanna's expression matched her son's. Billy lifted the revolver in his hands and fired off three shots. One struck the ceiling, sending a shower of plaster down on their heads; the other two punched through the door and the knocking stopped.

"Billy!" his mother screamed, but she could hardly hear her own voice over the ringing in her ears.

She clutched Joey to her chest and reached out to grab a hold of Billy as he ran by, grabbing the car keys off the counter as he passed. She missed, he didn't. He swung the door open and leapt over the deputy's body as he ran for his mother's car. Joanna heard the engine fire up and the tires squeal as Billy Parks sped off into the night.

***

The phones in the Tabor County Dispatch Center lit up and the lines started ringing. Nicole and Mandi grabbed the first two lines and Tina the next. The rest of the shift had gone home, all but Beth. She was doing a double-back and decided to sleep in the break room. Beth heard the commotion and ran into the comm center.

"What's going on?"

"Shots fired, grab a line," Tina said.

148

"9-1-1, what's your emergency?"

"I live up on Burns Court, and I just heard three gunshots."

"Are you sure they were—"

"I'm a hunter, and I know pistol shots when I hear 'em."

"Of course, I just meant with all the thunder out there—"

"Dammit, I know gunshots when I hear 'em! Now are you going to register my complaint or ain't you?"

"What's your address, sir?"

"Why the hell do you need my address?" the caller snapped. "The shooting ain't coming from my house."

"I understand, sir, but it might help us pinpoint where they came from."

"Pinpoint my ass! They came from the Parks's house. Then that boy, the older one, he's no good that one. He lit out like a bat out of hell in his mother's Corolla."

As the call came in, Tammy looked at the board and keyed her mic on channel three. "Deputy Rollins, status check. Deputy Rollins, status check."

The dispatchers all let the phones ring as they waited to hear Rollins respond to his status check. The check, like Lawson's, went unanswered.

***

Kevin Sullivan answered on the third ring and rubbed the sleep out of his eyes. He was the on-call detective with just seven hours to go on his turn in the barrel. What would it be tonight? Armed robbery at some all-night gas station, car burglar caught in the act, or God forbid, a home invasion? Those things, though few and far between, usually ended with either the offender or the homeowner getting shot, or, in some rare instances, both. Whatever it was, Sully knew that it meant climbing out of his warm bed and dragging his ass out to a crime scene.

"Yeah, Sully here."

"Kevin, it's Mandi...," she fell silent for a moment.

"Mandi?"

"It's Mike Rollins... just got shot."

Sully almost dropped his phone. "What happened, is he alive?"

"The medics are with him now. Sounds like he took one to the chest and one to the neck. It doesn't look good. I'm sorry, I know you guys were close."

Sully drew in a deep breath. He'd gone to the academy with Rollins. "Where?"

"5N751 Burns Court," she said. "I really am sorry, Kev."

"Thanks, Mandi, I'm heading out there now. Get

me on my portable if anything changes."

Sully ended the call and threw on the pair of jeans and the hoodie he'd worn earlier in the day. He slipped his belt through his holster, seated his Sig P320, and clipped on his badge. He flew down the stairs and out to his car and took off for 5N751 Burns Court. He knew the area well. There was a trailer park at the end of the road and the place gobbled up huge swaths of his time. By the time he got there, Burns Court was awash in a sea of flashing red-and-blue lights.

13

Chapter 13

Thursday, May 9, 2019
Oehlerking Farm, Rural Iowa

"We've checked the house and we know we're alone," Ray said. "I think it's best if we just barricade the door, make sure the windows are locked and hunker down here for the night. That storm isn't easing up."

Seneca adjusted her grip on the hatchet, chewed her lower lip and nodded in agreement. "I'll check the windows," she said.

Ray went to the front door to make sure the chair was still in place, and it was. Water was starting to blow in under the door right where he had dropped his bags and guitar when he had come back in. Not wanting his things getting any wetter, he dragged everything into the kitchen. Seneca was on her tiptoes checking the window locks above the sink. She turned and leaned against the sink, looked at him and smiled softly. In spite of himself, and the circumstances, Ray thought that he could get used to that view. Seneca leaning against the sink and looking at him that way. Not that he thought a woman's place was in the kitchen; Ray's father had done most of the cooking and all of the dishwashing. His dad never trusted dishwashers to do the job. It was just the sight of her that sat right with him. Then, out of nowhere, he heard the voice of Jack Traven, Keanu Reeves's character in the movie *Speed*. Jack told Annie, played by Sandra Bullock, that relationships based on intense experiences never work out. *Screw Jack Travern*, he thought to himself.

Seneca turned the knob and waited as the pipes buzzed and clattered and then spewed rust-colored water from the faucet. When the water finally cleared, she held the pot beneath the faucet. "You want some coffee? This guy has a shit-ton of coffee cans. half of them are still full."

She'd caught him in the middle of his thoughts.

"What?"

"Coffee; do you want some coffee?"

"You think that shit is safe to drink?"

"Should be. But I'll boil it just to make sure," she said. "Why are you looking at me like that?"

It wasn't his intention, but he must have been staring. "What do you mean? Like what?" Ray asked, knowing the answer.

She smiled softly. "Well, if I'm being honest..."

"By all means."

"Like a love-sick teenager," she answered.

Ray could feel his face get hot and could only imagine how red his cheeks must have been. "You like music?" he asked, eager to change the subject.

"Sure," she said. "Love it."

Ray snapped open the latches on his case and opened it on screeching hinges. He pulled the Arch-top from the case, set it on his lap, and fingered an A-chord to start The "Little Red Rooster" by Howlin Wolf, but it sounded like shit.

"Wow, so you carry that thing for show?" Seneca teased.

"Ha, ha. It's just out of tune."

Ray had just played it but it wasn't uncommon for a guitar to respond to shifts in temperature, though he'd never known his Gibson to be so sensitive. He tuned it up and began again. He managed to make it halfway through the song before the guitar went horribly out of tune again.

"Ouch," Seneca said. "Maybe you should stick to rescuing women."

Ray's brow furrowed. "What the hell?" He strummed the strings open and not one had stayed in tune. "I've never had this happen before," he said. Then he looked at his fingers. Orange lines ran across the tips. "Rust. How the hell could the strings be rusting already?"

"Well," Seneca said. "It doesn't sound like you practice much."

She offered a playful smile, but Ray didn't return it. Instead, he stared at his hand, working the fingers back and forth. A deep frown formed on his face. The ringing in his ears was coming in ebbs and flows and his knuckles throbbed.

"What's wrong, Ray?"

"It's my fingers, they hurt so bad."

Seneca turned off the stove and walked over. "Let me see."

She took hold of Ray's hand and he winced. His knuckles were red and beginning to swell. "Do you have arthritis?"

"I'm twenty-four, how can I have arthritis?"

"I'll admit it's very rare, but not unheard of. How long has it been bothering you?"

Ray looked at his watch. It had stopped running at 9:00 PM. "That's weird, this thing never stops," he said, tapping the crystal.

"How long, Ray?"

"I don't know, just a few hours I guess."

Seneca shook her head. "That's impossible." She turned his hand over in hers and probed the joints with her thumb.

Ray jerked his hand back and sucked air through his teeth. "Ouch! What are you doing?"

"Ray, you have advanced arthritis in your hand. It must have been troubling you for years."

"Well, I don't know what to tell you, but I have never had any trouble with my hands. And I can play the shit out of this thing." He held the Gibson proudly by the neck.

Seneca took his hand back in hers; he offered it with no hesitation. "I'm surprised you can even move your fingers. Hang on." She grabbed her t-shirt that she'd been using for a rag. She dipped it in the boiling water, rung it out, and placed the warm compress across his knuckles.

Relief came slowly, but it came. "That feels better, thanks," Ray said. "But I don't understand, how can I develop arthritis just like that?" He snapped the fingers on his other hand and cried out. The pain was instantaneous. "What's happening to me?"

"I don't know," Seneca said. "I've never heard of rapid-onset arthritis."

As the words left her lips, Ray noticed Seneca's eyes widen. "What's wrong?"

"Open and close your mouth for me."

Ray did as he was asked.

"Now rotate your head around."

Seneca demonstrated and Ray obliged. "I don't get it."

"Maybe I didn't sterilize the needle enough. It could be tetanus, but that usually takes a couple of weeks to develop. Have you cut yourself recently, or maybe had a blister that burst and got infected?"

"No, not that I can think of."

"What's that on the back of your hand?" Seneca asked, pointing at the wound Ray had sustained while searching for car keys under the front seat of Oehlerking's car.

"That's nothing, just a scratch I got while I was trying to get you out of the trunk."

Seneca patted the wound with the warm towel. "It doesn't look too bad," she said, and then checked his ear again. "Shit, Ray, your ear looks infected. We have to get you to a hospital. We need to get you on an antibiotic, and I want to run some tests."

A thunder clap shook the little house and rain battered the roof and windows.

"I don't think we're going anywhere for a while," Ray said.

"It's just rain Ray. If we don't get you looked at you run the risk of developing sepsis."

"Rain and a psycho lurking out there in the dark!"

Seneca touched his cheek. "You're looking pale," she said, and took his wrist.

"What are you doing?"

"Shh, I'm checking your pulse. She turned her own wrist to look at her watch. "What the hell?"

"What is it?"

"My watch, it stopped." She readjusted her fingers and felt for his pulse. "Do you feel dizzy, light headed?"

Ray wobbled his head from side to side. "I don't know, not really."

"I'm not feeling a strong pulse, Ray. Sepsis can cause a drop in blood pressure. It's called septic shock and it can cause organ failure." As the words came out of her mouth she shook her head. "But that's impossible. It can't happen that fast."

"I'm fine," Ray insisted. Look, for now, this is the safest place for us. We've locked the door and checked the house. Believe me, we're safer inside than out there."

"You're probably right," she agreed. "I'm just worried about that wound."

"Of course, I'm right," he said, in his most reassuring voice. "As soon as the sun comes up, we'll get out of here, but for now we're safe and dry."

Seneca frowned. "I guess."

"Why don't you pull the other chair over here?" Ray turned his chair so that she could get closer. "You can rest your head against my shoulder and maybe get some sleep. I'll take first watch," Ray suggested. "In the morning, we'll head down the road and look for help."

"What about the coffee?"

"I don't think we should be eating or drinking anything while we're here. You know, just to be on the safe side."

"I guess you're right," she said, sliding the chair over.

She laid her head against his chest and Ray wrapped his arms around her. He was holding her again and he liked it. He stroked her head softly even though the contact made his hands hurt. He looked down at her and could see right down her zipped up hoodie. Ray averted his eyes and fought the urge to glance down whenever it came. That battle kept him distracted until exhaustion overtook him.

***

The dark thing slipped through the gap under the front door, dragging the cold from the storm with it. It made no sound as it moved like ground fog across the hall and through the kitchen. It passed right over Ray's and Seneca's legs, causing both to stir but not to waken. The dark thing moved to the foot of the stairs and crawled silently up into the shadows of the second floor.

159

Chapter 14

Friday, May 10, 2019
Tabor County, Iowa

The windshield wipers beat rhythmically, and Kevin Sullivan let out a long, slow sigh. He would never admit it; hell, he wouldn't even say it out loud to himself, but he suffered serious bouts of imposter syndrome. He had never planned to be a police officer, it had happened almost by accident. He had been sitting at the lunch counter at Khoury's Drug Store on break from his job at the Quick Lube. Thumbing through the newspaper, he came across an ad for the sheriff's department. It said that the applicants needed to be between 21 and 36, with no criminal record and a high school diploma or equivalent. That was it. No college degree, no previous law enforcement experience, just a clean record, and a diploma. He was 24, check, had a clean record, check, and his GED, so he stopped at the Tabor County Sheriff's Department after work and filled out an application. That was six years ago. He worked at the jail and the courthouse for a while and had only been on the road for three years when the Sheriff stuck him in the investigative division. He'd barely gotten his feet wet as a patrolman, and now here he was, working what — a murder investigation? Not to mention that the victim was a police officer. The very definition of one being out over their skis.

Sully got out of his car and keyed his mic. "Dispatch, Detective Sullivan is 10-23."

"10-04, Detective, we have you on scene. Please switch over to channel three," Tammy replied.

Sully switched his radio knob over to channel three, pushed his way past the group of onlookers, and approached the first face he recognized.

"Jake," he said, addressing Deputy Jake Pool. "How's it going?"

Deputy Pool had been on the job for sixteen years and, despite putting in for Investigations several times, had never moved out of the patrol division. But to his credit, he wasn't pissy about it like some of the other veterans. Sully was a fast-tracker, and everyone knew it. The guy had a nose for finding shit, and he led the department in drug arrests his first year out of field training. In his second year on the job, Sully turned a simple drug arrest into a break on a sex traffic ring, and from there, the sky was the limit.

"Hey Kev," Jake greeted him somberly. "What a fucking night, huh? First Lawson and now this."

"What do we know?" Sully asked, completely missing the part about Lawson.

"It's really fucking bad. Mikey's on his way to Lutheran General, took one in the neck." Jake closed his eyes and shook his head. "It's really fucking bad, man."

"Do we know who the shooter is?"

Jake nodded toward one of the houses. "That's the shooter's mom and little brother."

"The shooter's a kid?"

"Fifteen. He shot Mikey right through the fucking door and tore ass out of here in his mom's Corolla."

Sully broke out his notepad and began writing, doing his best to keep the pages from getting wet. "Did we get an attempt-to-locate out for the vehicle and shooter?"

"Yeah, did that right after we checked the house for the kid."

"And did we mention that the shooter is a kid?"

"Fuck if I know, Cantore put the call in to dispatch."

"I just don't want any cowboy shit. I'm sure the kid's running scared."

Deputy Cantore was new to the force and still with his field training officer. FTO Jeff Anderson. Anderson was as squared away as they came. Deep-set eyes, a strong chin, the kind of face that said; don't even bother telling me a joke. Sully knew Anderson would make sure the kid did everything by the book, and that took a little of the pressure off.

"Okay, Jake, I'll catch you later."

"Shit like this makes me glad I didn't make detective."

Sully smiled uncomfortably. "It's not all it's cracked up to be, brother."

He lifted the crime scene tape and slipped under. Burns Court was an old and not well-maintained blacktop road; it was more gravel than tar in most places, so the puddles were plentiful, and Sully did his best to avoid them. He hopped from semi-dry patch to semi-dry patch because there were few things he loathed more than wet feet. He walked up to the porch where the woman and her son were seated. Cantore and FTO Anderson were standing nearby. Cantore turned to greet him.

"Detective Sullivan, good—" he paused, probably not sure what to call it. Evening, morning, either way, it sure as shit was not good.

"Cantore, Anderson," Sully regarded each with a nod.

Anderson tipped his cap. "Excuse me for a minute, would ya? I want to check on Deputy Pool."

"Of course," Sully replied.

"Detective Sullivan, this is Joanna and Joey Parks," Cantore said, motioning to the two sopping wet mother and son.

Joanna bolted to her feet. "You're the detective?"

"Yes, ma'am."

"Did they find my son?"

"Not yet, at least not as far as I am aware. Can you tell me what happened?"

Joey opened his mouth, but Joanna shot him a stern look, and he closed it quickly.

"You have something you want to say, son?"

"He's not your son, and I suppose you already know that his father is in prison."

"I apologize, and no, I didn't know that," Sully said. "Is it okay if I call you..." He referred to his notebook. "Joey?"

"Sure, Mr. Sullivan."

"It's Detective Sullivan," Cantore barked.

Joey Parks leaned away like a batter dodging a brushback heater.

Sully bent over, his hands on his knees. "It's okay Joey, how about you just call me Sully? That's what most people call me."

"Look, Mr. Sullivan," Joanna shot Cantore an angry glare, "this guy won't let me and my son back into our house. I know my rights, and I know you can't keep me out of my house without a warrant."

"Well, ma'am, the fact is, we *can* keep you out. It's called exigent circumstances. That means—"

"I know what exigent means," she interrupted.

Sully smiled warmly. "Of course you do. I'm sorry."

"They aren't even doing anything, this guy—" she waved a dismissive hand at Cantore "—is just standing there with his thumb up his ass."

Sully opened his mouth to speak, but this time it was Cantore who interrupted. "We're waiting for the evidence techs to get here, and for your information, we are getting a warrant signed by a judge as we speak. So, we can keep you out as long as we want."

Sully walked up onto the porch past Joanna and her son, got face to face with Cantore and spoke calmly through gritted teeth. "Take a walk."

"But she..."

Sully exhaled slowly and relaxed his jaw. "I know. But please." Sully extended a hand, directing Cantore down the stairs and toward the street. Cantore took the cue.

Sully sat down on the step next to Joanna. "I'm

sorry about that, Mrs. Parks. He can be a little gruff, but he's right...well, not about keeping you out as long as we want. We can only prevent you from entering for as long as needed, but we'll do our best not to inconvenience you any longer than is absolutely necessary. How's that sound?"

Sully offered a disarming smile. Joanna's shoulders fell, her head dropped, and she began to cry. "I'm sorry, I just can't believe any of this is real."

"Is there anything you can tell me that might help us find your son?"

Joanna cast angry eyes up at Sully. "Why, so you can shoot him?"

"No, ma'am, just the opposite. The sooner we bring this to a close, the safer your boy will be. Suppose you start by telling me his name?"

"She won't tell me," Cantore called from the sidewalk, "and she won't let the boy tell me either."

Looking past the detective, Joanna barked. "That's because you're an asshole!" Then softening her tone, she turned her attention back toward Sully. "His name is Billy — well, William, but we all call him Billy. He's a good boy, Detective. I just don't understand any of this." Joanna wrapped her arms around herself.

"I'm sure he is," Sully said and carefully placed a comforting hand on her shoulder. "I promise you; we'll do our best to bring him home safely. Can you tell me where Billy got the gun?"

Joanna shook her head. "I don't know. We don't own any guns."

Joey leaned over and whispered in his mother's ear, and her eyes went wide.

"What did he say?" Sully asked.

"He said —" she paused, and it looked to Sully like she was trying to make sense of what her son had just told her. "— he said that Billy took it from the man in the woods."

Sully leaned closer to Joey. "What man in the woods?"

"The deputy," Joey whispered.

"Deputy?"

"Well, he's wearing a uniform, like that." He pointed at Cantore.

Cantore dropped the flashlight he'd been holding. It fell to the ground and went out. Anderson, who had just returned from checking on Deputy Pool, shouldered past him.

"What deputy are you talking about, son? Where is he?"

"There's a deputy in the woods. Billy took the gun from his belt."

"Is the deputy..." he searched for the right word, "hurt?" Anderson asked.

Sully heard the quiver in Anderson's voice. The mercury vapor lamps that hung from the light poles gave off an eerie green tone that hung in the mist, and Sully thought that Anderson looked like he was going to vomit.

"What am I missing here?" Sully asked.

"Deputy Lawson went missing earlier today," Anderson answered. "We all just assumed that his radio went out. You know how they do."

Sully thought it sounded like Anderson was seeking absolution.

"He stopped answering his radio checks after dinner," Anderson explained.

Fuck! One dead deputy and one hanging on to life, Sully thought.

"Everybody's been out looking." Umber crept up Anderson's neck and settled in his cheeks.

"Why wasn't I notified? I'm the on-call!"

"Not my call to make, Sully."

"Fuck!"

Sully knew he shouldn't have snapped at his old friend, but he hated surprises, especially when they involved his investigations, and this was certainly his case. "Where is the deputy, Joey? Can you take us to him?"

Joey shook his head, slowly at first and then faster. "No, I can't."

"It could be a matter of life and death. We might still be able to save him."

"No, you can't. He's dead. Besides, I don't

remember where he is. My brother found him."

"Did Billy kill him? Is that why you don't want to take us out there?" Sully demanded.

"What? No!"

"He said he doesn't remember where the body is!" Joanna was on her feet and in Sully's face. "We've been cooperative, but we've been sitting here in the rain for over half a fucking hour! We're going inside!"

"You step one foot off this porch, and I'll slam your ass behind bars and turn Joey over to child protective services. Now sit the fuck down," Cantore ordered.

Joanna flinched and did as she was told. Sully had seen that kind of response before. It was the way his mother reacted when his father yelled at her. "I'm sorry, Joanna, but there is a deputy somewhere who needs help, and Joey is the only one who can help him."

Joanna didn't move or say a word. She didn't even make eye contact with Sully. Joey clung to his mother and stared daggers at the detective. Cantore had gone too far in threatening to take the boy away from his mother. If Joey was being honest, and Sully had no reason to think he wasn't, Joey Parks was their best bet at locating the missing lawman.

Fists clenched and breathing heavily, Joanna glared at Cantore. Once again, Sully would have to undo the damage done to the rapport he had been cultivating with Joanna Parks. "Joey, Joanna, I want to apologize for Deputy Cantore. He shouldn't have yelled at you, and he certainly," he emphasized the word certainly, "shouldn't have threatened you. I'm sure his FTO will be detailing that in his report, but right now I really need your help."

Sully had deliberately chosen the word I rather than we in an effort to separate himself from the deputies. The tactic seemed to have worked. Joey looked at his mother and nodded. "I can help, Mom."

Joanna turned away from Cantore and closed her eyes for a moment. "Fine, but if that asshole says another word to me or my son—" "—I can assure you, Mrs. Parks, he won't," Sully promised and directed his attention to Joey. "Did your brother do something to the deputy?"

"Yes, sir," Joey said, and cast his eyes downward.

"What did he do, Joey?"

"He took his gun, and he was—" Joey tugged at his shirt. "—touching him."

"What do you mean, touching him?"

Joey touched his belly with his fingertips. "Like his guts. He was touching his guts."

The words corkscrewed into Sully's brain. He couldn't imagine what that looked like. A person's guts were tucked away, all nice and neat, on the inside of their body. In what version of reality would Lawson's guts be exposed to be touched by a little boy? He wanted to speak, but nothing was coming out. Luckily, Joanna found her tongue again.

"Did Billy kill the deputy?" she asked.

"No, Mom, we found him like that."

"Is that why you felt sick? Why you didn't want me to go to work?"

"Yeah. I wanted you to stay with me."

She took her son's head in her hands and locked eyes with the thin little boy. "Joey, so help me God, I will never leave you alone when you need me. Never again, baby." She hugged him to her chest.

"I'm not a baby, Mom. And I think I can show the officers where the body is."

Sully stopped trying to imagine the scene and re-joined the conversation. "I would really appreciate that, Joey. You and your mother can ride with me."

"I don't think I could find it in a car. We gotta walk."

"I'm coming with," said Anderson. "Cantore," now it was Anderson who spoke through gritted teeth, "you stay here and don't let anyone in that house. Our ETs should be here soon. Yell over to Pool if you need anything or get me on channel four."

Sully led them through the crowd and stopped

at his car. He pulled an umbrella from the trunk and handed it to Joanna. She was already soaked to the bone but accepted the gesture. She thumbed the button, and the umbrella opened with a great swoosh. It was a huge golf umbrella and could have sheltered all four of them, but Sully and Anderson stayed out.

"It's about a forty-five-minute walk," Joey said. "Is that okay?"

It's going to have to be, Sully thought and nodded. "Yeah, Joey. Whatever it takes, buddy."

15

Chapter 15

Friday, May 10, 2019
Oehlerking Farm – Rural, Iowa

I t wasn't the first time that the dark thing had brought Rodney back from death. It had happened once before when Rodney was just a little boy. The Oehlerkings were pig farmers, and Rodney despised the noisy, smelly animals. He'd always felt that his father preferred their company to his, but Rodney hadn't dared to bring up hurt feelings with his father. One didn't trouble a man like Henry Oehlerking with such things. Instead, Rodney took his aggression out on the source of his pain. His favorite way of punishing the animals for stealing his father's attention was to go out to the pens with his slingshot. Rodney would find the roughest rocks he could, set them in the leather pocket, draw back good and hard, and let fly. It would send the animals into a rage, and he thought it was a hoot. His father would have beaten the tar out of him if he'd ever got caught, so Rodney would only do it when his father ran into town.

One hot and still August afternoon, Henry found himself in need of chicken wire to repair a hole in the coop. He asked Rodney if he wanted to take a ride, but Rodney declined. When his father pulled out of the driveway, he ran into the house, grabbed his slingshot, and hurried over to the big pen, the one that housed the boars. Rodney hated the boars most of all, and they hated him right back. The whole pen would get riled up at the very sight of the boy. Rodney perched himself up on the fence and began snapping off shot after shot at the huge, tusked swine. He'd gotten off perhaps nine or ten shots when he heard his father call out.

"What the hell are you doing?" Henry shouted.

Hearing his father's voice, Rodney spun, and in doing so, lost his balance and fell flat on his back on the wrong side of the fence. The boar was on him in no time. Its tusk pierced Rodney's right eye as the beast stomped and chewed his antagonizer. Before Henry could intervene, the powerful animal had ripped the right side of his son's face to ribbons and crushed his spine. As he flowed in and out of consciousness, he'd heard his father tell his mother, Harriet, that he had forgotten his wallet and returned home to retrieve it. The wild squealing of his herd sent him running to the pens for fear that some predator had wandered in among the drove.

Rodney's mother begged his father to take him into town to see a doctor, but Henry refused. As part of the Watch Tower Society, his religion forbade what he called the blood sciences. Instead, he took Rodney up to the spare room, laid him on a blanket on the floor, and prayed. Harriet wanted to put him in his bed, but Henry said no one would buy a bed that a boy had died in.

Henry prayed night and day over his son, but infection set in and Rodney's health continued to worsen. He ran a fever, no one knew how high: the Oehlerkings didn't own a thermometer, but the infection spread quickly and the fever wouldn't break. Within a few days, it was clear that he would not survive his injuries, and Henry retreated to the shed to build a proper box for the boy. Harriet sought other remedies. Since it seemed that God wasn't going to answer her prayers, she turned her plea to one who might. The night Rodney passed, Harriet offered herself in exchange for her boy's life.

She had no book to follow, no one to lead her, only a burning desire that her child be saved. As

Henry slept, Harriet moved on cat's feet into the spare room. They'd always planned on a larger family, but the Lord didn't see fit to bless them with any more children. She entered the room where Rodney lay dead on the floor and lit an oil lamp. As a child, her mother warned her of the dangers of the world outside the church. She taught about the principalities of the Evil One. She instructed her to beware of covens and demonic signs, pentagrams, inverted crosses, and the like, so Harriet put her limited knowledge to work. She pierced her finger with the large needle she used for mending Henry's workwear, and the blood came quickly. Dragging her finger over her son's forehead, Harriet drew a crude pentagram and then did her best to mirror the image on her own forehead. By the time she'd finished, her blood was getting sticky and hard to work. She opened another hole in her finger and finished by drawing inverted crosses and the number of the beast across both of their faces.

She prayed a blasphemous prayer and lay on the floor next to her son. Having made her offer as best she could, she could think of nothing more to do, so she slept. Harriet was awoken by the presence of another in the room. The glow from the oil lamp cast the room in warm yellow light, and Harriet searched the dark corners but saw only Rodney, cold and blue. Believing she'd imagined it, Harriet lay back down.

As she slept a fitful sleep, she dreamed that a tiny seed settled into the pit of her stomach. The seed took root and blossomed into a dark thing that rolled and churned in her belly and woke her with intense cramping. The pain brought her to her knees. She hadn't eaten in days, and her stomach was empty, save for this dark thing. She could feel it clawing at her insides trying to get out. The movement caused her stomach to spasm, and she doubled over. Her diaphragm convulsed violently as the dark thing wormed its way up through her esophagus and crawled slick with bile from her mouth.

Now it was out. Harriet rocked back on her heels and wiped her lips as the evil she had just spat into existence scurried rat-like across the floor to sit upon her dead son's chest. She reached out to pull the thing back, but it was too late. Black tendrils flowed into her son's nose and vanished into his body.

Harriet wept and pulled her hair. Shame, remorse, and self-loathing enveloped her like a blanket even as she watched her dead son open his one remaining eye. Rodney blinked, looking to her like a person suddenly finding that they could breathe underwater... or perhaps finding themselves on the surface of some planet wholly foreign. Rodney sat up, sucked in a breath, and cried out in agony.

The boy made a quick recovery, but as Rodney grew stronger, his mother began to fail. It wasn't her body. Physically, there was nothing noticeably wrong; no fever, good color, but her mental capacities began to rapidly decline. She mumbled incantations in a strange tongue and began carving unrecognizable symbols deep into her flesh. Henry locked his wife in the spare room and returned to prayer. The end came quickly. That night, only three days after Rodney's incident with the boar, Harriet Oehlerking hung herself in the same room where she had struck her wicked deal.

Now, as the dark thing brought Rodney back for a second time, it was he who found himself twirling lazily at the end of his mother's rope. He felt the noose tighten under his weight and he worked his fingers in between the skin of his neck and the thick horsehair. Being much taller than his mother, Rodney found that the tips of his toes touched the ground. It wasn't much, but it was enough to keep from dying of strangulation.

16

Chapter 16

Friday, May 10, 2019
Rural – Iowa

The taillights on the truck ahead blurred with each passing of the Corolla's shitty wiper blades, and Billy had to squint to see them. He yawned and shook his head. The adrenaline dump he got after shooting the deputy and stealing his mother's car had sapped his energy, and the steady patter of the rain and beating of the wipers wasn't going to help him stay awake. He wanted to pull over and sleep, but that was out of the question, so he cranked the radio, opened the window, and pressed on.

Billy's father taught him how to drive as soon as he was tall enough to work the pedals. He hadn't had much practice since his father went up on his third DUI. Lucky for him, Iowa wasn't a three-strike state, and he would only have to do three years of his five-year sentence. Still, that meant another eight months behind bars, and by the looks of things, Billy might just be starting his stretch when his old man was getting out. But that was only if he got caught, and he didn't plan on letting that happen.

Adding to his problems was the fact that the Corolla only had one working headlight. Aside from making it harder to see, it also provided probable cause for a cop to stop him. He'd learned that from the TV show Cops. He also knew about APBs. Not so much what the letters stood for, but that every cop in the state would be looking for him once the APB got out. He decided that he had to get off Route 63, so took the next right onto an old dirt road.

Dauberman Road was a seven-mile stretch of potholes, which was great, because most people avoided it. It was also great because it led to a number of switchbacks and turn offs that even a local could get lost on. And getting lost was exactly what Billy had in mind.

The bouncing tires cleared his head for the moment, and he decided to flick through the radio stations for any news about him or the officer he shot. As he turned the dial, a strange thought occurred to him. He supposed that he should have been hoping for the officer to pull through, but he wasn't. He loved the thought of having killed a cop. He was willing to bet that he would be a hero in the joint. But still, it ran counter to his strong desire for self-preservation, and he had to consider the fact that he might have screwed up.

Billy had always operated under the assumption that whatever he did was all right. He never got in trouble for anything: not for killing the neighbor's cat, not for breaking his brother's arm, not for the myriad other things he had done. So, as long as he could scratch his itch without consequence, why not scratch away? But this time was different. This time it was going to cost him. He supposed it was his mother's fault for never holding him account-able. There was a time when he'd considered killing her, especially after his father got locked up. She was in the car with them when his father veered off the road and hit the tree. He begged her to switch seats with him before the cops showed up, but she refused. She got the back of his hand for that one, but she sat there in her seat like the stubborn bitch she was and let him take the rap. Man, how he wanted to kill her after that, but he didn't. He didn't because he knew the cops would have sent him and Joey to live with their aunt and uncle, a couple of ball-busting Bible-thumpers, and he wasn't about to put up with their bullshit.

Since turning onto Dauberman, Billy had spent the better part of thirty minutes splashing in and out of potholes, but he could still see the lights from the trucks buzzing down the main road. Dauberman ran west for a short distance and then turned and paralleled Highway 63. He didn't know exactly where he was, but he still knew the area, and that meant he had to get farther away. As he bounced along, a flash of lightning lit the sky, and Billy could see that the road curved up ahead. He exhaled a sigh of relief. He figured the curve would take him away from the main roads, and that's where he needed to go. But the relief was short-lived. As he rounded the bend, the old Corolla began to chug, and then died. He glanced at the gas-gauge.

"Fuck! Stupid bitch! She can't even keep gas in the tank!"

Billy slammed his palm against the steering wheel and rubbed his forehead. He needed a new plan. *Across the field, back toward 63, there was bound to be a gas station,* he thought. Billy pulled the revolver, feeling the weight in his hands, and mentally counted the shots he had taken. There was the guy he'd come across in the woods when he and Joey went back out to look at the deputy's body. In Billy's defense, he thought the guy might have been the one who killed the deputy. But when he went to make sure he was dead, he saw the letterman jacket and figured he was just some stupid-ass jock cutting home through the woods. "Wrong place at the wrong time," Billy said to himself. Then there was the deputy who came to his house. Billy figured he was there to arrest him, so he had to shoot him. *Was that two or three shots at the deputy?* He couldn't be sure, but either way, he knew he had at least two, best case, three bullets left.

There was no telling how long he would be out on his own, so he had to start thinking about food and shelter. He couldn't risk staying in the car; that was for damned sure. All it would take was for him to fall asleep and for some cop to roll up on him. He would be a sitting duck.

Billy rummaged through the glove compartment and took what he thought might be useful: a flashlight, some Handi-Wipes, some gum, and a lighter. His mom always carried a roll of toilet paper in the center console, and he grabbed that too, just in case. He crammed the lighter, Handi-Wipes, and the gum into his pocket and clicked on the flashlight to make sure it worked. The light was dim, so Billy gave it a good hard whack. It brightened right up. He pointed it up into the rainy sky and stared, momentarily mesmerized by the droplets of water falling toward the beam. Satisfied that it worked, Billy turned it off and started walking. Maybe he'd get lucky and be able to carjack some jerk while he was filling up. If not, he figured he could just kill the attendant and then take all the food and pop he could carry. One thing was for sure; Billy would have wheels, food, or both.

17

Chapter 17

Friday, May 10, 2019
Oehlerking Farm – Rural Iowa

Rodney strained against the coarse rope until his head slipped free of the noose and he fell to the floor. He worked the soreness in his jaw and could taste wet earth in the back of his throat. He coughed hoarsely and blinked clarity into his eyes. But as soon as his eyes cleared, he wished they hadn't. Rodney lay flat on his back, staring with unblinking eyes as his mother's noose swayed above where the dark thing had deposited him. A chill ran through him. He had hung, at last count, twenty-eight different women from that noose but had never experienced it for himself. A deep, abiding sadness ran through him, and he wept into his large, calloused hands. He wept for the women, each of whom had failed the test that it seemed he himself had just passed, and he wept for his mother.

The day before she passed, Harriet had called him into her sewing room. She had just made the most beautiful white linen gown and said that she wanted Rodney's opinion before showing his father. Naturally, Rodney obliged. While they sat together, Harriet told him that she would be leaving him soon. Rodney told her that he didn't really understand what she meant. She told him not to worry; she merely told him that he was to look for her in her next life. Then she kissed him lightly on his cheek and sent him away. The next morning, Rodney found his mother swinging, neck broken, from the rope that now dangled above him.

Henry Oehlerking burst into the room, perhaps drawn by his son's mournful wailing. Being the hard and serious man that he was, he took her body down and buried it out on their property. At twelve, Rodney was already taller than his mother, so Henry took the box he'd built for his son and laid his wife's body inside. Together with his son, they dug a grave. Then, without so much as a tear or a word of prayer, they lowered the casket into the ground and covered it up. Rodney asked his father why he wouldn't let him pray over her. Henry said that he would not dishonor God further by speaking the words. He told Rodney that his mother would burn in Hell for all eternity for what she had done. Rodney asked if God ever gave second chances; his father told him that it was too late for second chances once you were dead.

"You got to make your peace with the Creator every day, boy," Henry said. "'Cause the day you don't will be a day too late."

Henry left that room exactly as he'd found it and told Rodney that he was never to go back in there. And Rodney had obeyed, right up until a month after his dad died, when he began feeling lonely. Rodney cleared his head of the memory, got into a seated position and pressed his hands flat on the floor, and his house spoke to him. *There was someone else here. They had been right here in this very room*, he thought. No matter. He knew they were still somewhere in his web.

* * *

The loud thud from the second floor woke Seneca. She froze and perked her ears, hoping to God that it had been her imagination. Then she heard what sounded like a cough, and she knew. She moved as quietly as she could and pushed herself out of Ray's arms, trying not to startle him awake. But it seemed that Ray hadn't been able to sleep too deeply either.

"Hey," he said softly. "Why's it so fucking hot in here?" he asked, tugging at his sweat-drenched T-shirt as the radiator pinged softly in the corner.

Seneca pressed her finger to her lips. "Shh." Then she pointed up.

From somewhere in the dark on the second floor, a floorboard squeaked. Seneca reached for the hatchet, but it was gone. She whipped her head around. It had been there when she closed her eyes; she was sure of it. Seneca turned back toward Ray. He was gripping the handle of the hatchet so tightly that his knuckles had turned white.

"That's mine," she said hesitantly.

Ray cocked his head as if he were listening very carefully to someone speaking, only the someone wasn't her. He began to reach forward as if to offer the weapon and then clutched it to his chest. Seneca took a step back, unsure of what was happening. As she watched, Ray pressed his eyes shut and shook his head violently.

"Shut up! Just shut up!"

"Who are you talking to?"

Ray didn't answer. He just kept shaking his head and repeating the words, "Shut up, shut up," like a mantra.

"Ray, you're scaring me. Please stop!"

Instinctively, she reached for the pot and cocked it back to swing. She'd backed clear to the sink, but

Ray didn't follow. He just stood, hatchet in hand, whipping his head back and forth and side to side like a can in a paint shaker.

Then he stopped shaking. "Shut the fuck up!" he shouted.

A sound like a heavy duffel bag falling from a high shelf came from the floor above, and Ray looked like he'd just woken from a nightmare.

"Ray, are you okay?"

"I don't know. Something's happening to me," he said as he slammed the heel of his hand into the side of his head.

"We have to get the fuck out of here," Seneca insisted. "There's someone upstairs!"

Something between a yell and a growl erupted from the second floor. Without a word, Seneca and Ray ran for the door. Ray turned the knob and pulled, but the door didn't budge.

"The deadbolt!" she yelled as she glanced over her shoulder at the staircase.

Ray snapped the deadbolt with a loud click. Above them, heavy footsteps crossed the floor in the direction of the staircase. Seneca's hand collided with Ray's as they both reached for the knob. Ray turned it, and they both pulled, but the door still wouldn't budge. The rain seemed to have swollen the wood and pinched the door against the jamb.

"Pull harder!" Seneca screamed.

"I'm pulling as hard as I can!"

But the door wouldn't move. Then Ray spoke in a voice that Seneca didn't recognize.

"Fuck the bitch, let the old man have her. You get your skinny white ass outta here!"

Seneca staggered back. "Ray?"

"The name's Bones, baby. And I guess your name is mud?" he said and laughed madly, like he'd just delivered a gut-buster of a punchline.

As he laughed, the skin on his face mottled and wrinkled. Large cords stood out on his neck, and his Adam's apple swelled to the size of a pool ball. Seneca tightened her grip on the pot handle. A black fog rolled across the floor and began crawling its way up Ray's legs, and when she looked back up at his face, it had changed. The kind but sad face that she had only known for a few hours was replaced by something frightening, something dangerous.

The warrior in Seneca pushed past her fear, and she flew into a rage. She swung the heavy pot with everything she had, connecting with the side of Ray's head. He fell hard against the door, and the hatchet dropped from his hand. Seneca grabbed Ray by the hair, dragged him away from the door, and smashed him one more time with the pot. Then she picked up the hatchet and swung hard at the door. The wood splintered with each blow, and in less than a minute, Seneca had chopped a hole in the center of the door, but it was taking too long. Whoever or whatever was upstairs was coming, and she had to get out. She began kicking at the door and finally heard a great crack as a large section of the lower panel fell away. Wind and rain swept in through the opening, and Seneca could see freedom just ahead.

* * *

Rodney exited the room as quickly as he could and made his way over to the staircase. His legs felt wobbly, but after all, he'd just been brought back from the dead. He braced himself on the banister and set one unsteady foot down the first stair. He tried to call out to whoever was in his house, but it came in a raspy caw, his throat having just suffered the trauma of near strangulation. Rodney brought his second foot to the same stair and stepped down again. It was slow and painful going, but he had to get down there. It sounded like they were busting his place all to hell.

* * *

Seneca stepped her leg through the opening she'd made in the door. It was wide enough for her to fit through, but just barely. She was halfway through when she felt someone grab hold of her foot. She stomped down hard to try to break free, but it was no use. Whatever had her wasn't letting go. She tried again, but this time she got pulled against the door. Her head slammed into the wood. In a daze, Seneca twisted her body, placed both hands on the door frame, and pushed. She broke free and heard Ray call her name before a great commotion erupted inside the house. Seneca landed hard on the porch.

She scrambled to her feet and sprinted down the driveway. When she reached the road, she stopped. She couldn't just leave him. Ray had risked his own life to save hers. He could have left her in the trunk and made a run for it, but he didn't. Somehow, he managed to get the better of her captor, busted her out of the trunk, and then did his best to keep her safe. And what had she done for him? Sure, she sewed up his ear, but that was only after she'd cracked him in the side of the head with the tire iron, nearly ripping it off in the first place. And who knows, maybe whatever was wrong was some brain injury that she had caused when she hit him.

"Shit!"

She approached the front door and got low enough to try to see inside the house. She had dropped the hatchet when she climbed through the hole, a choice she now regretted. She had to find it, go back in there, and try to save Ray. He'd managed to take the old man out once all on his own, she thought. Now it would be two against one, and she liked those odds.

"I'm coming, Ray!"

* * *

Rodney crossed the floor toward Ray, who was just getting back to his feet. As he neared the intruder, he felt a heavy thud as the pot smashed against the side of his head. His brain told his knees to buckle, but something inside managed to keep him upright. Rodney swung his big, knotted fist into Ray's jaw, knocking him out cold and sending him sprawling across the floor. Rodney stood over Ray for a moment and then lifted him, tossed him onto his shoulder and carried Ray up to the sewing room, where he set about binding his hands and feet.

193

18

Chapter 18

Friday, May 10, 2019
Oehlerking Farm – Rural Iowa

Seneca braced herself and stepped back into the house. There was an eerie silence on the first floor. Just a moment ago it sounded like a brawl but now all was quiet; even the radiator had ceased its relentless pinging. She felt around for the hatchet where she'd dropped it, afraid to lower her eyes, but it was gone. *Maybe Ray picked it up?* she thought to herself. She swallowed hard and called out softly.

"Ray — Ray, where are you?"

A loud thud overhead drew her attention, and she crossed over to the staircase as quietly as she could. She clenched her fists and considered that she might just have to fight the old man. Then she remembered the strength in his hands when he grabbed her. Big, powerful hands. She had tried to break free, but he was just too strong. Stepping over to the drawer where Ray had found the silverware, Seneca pulled the butter knife and fork and wrapped her hands tightly around them.

"This is stupid, this is stupid, this is stupid," she said over and over. She knew the smart thing to do was to run. Perhaps she could make it to the neighbors house where she could call the police. Maybe she could even borrow the guy's shotgun and run back here. Seneca shook her head. She knew she was just trying to justify leaving Ray behind, and she pushed the thought away. She searched the first floor and found she was alone. Seneca knew what she had to do. She was going to have to go up those stairs, and rescue her friend. She held the knife and fork out in front of her and started up. The stairs creaked as she climbed them one by one. They seemed to go on forever, and about halfway up, Seneca began thinking that she'd made the wrong decision. She considered going back down but was afraid to turn her back on the darkness above. Seneca paused at the middle stair and fought back her fear.

"You can do this, Seneca," she said to herself. "He's only a man, and a fucking old man, at that. Get your ass up and go save your friend."

Her pep talk seemed to work because she was

up off of her ass. At the top of the stairs, the short wall blocked her view. She couldn't see what she was up against without exposing herself. Seneca considered the possibility that she may have imagined the sounds she'd heard from the second floor, but either way, she knew she wouldn't be alone up there. If nothing else, Ray had to have gone up there since he wasn't downstairs and he hadn't come out the front door after her. And that was a big part of what worried her. She didn't want to accidentally stab her friend.

"Ray," she called out again, but her whisper went unanswered.

Seneca paused a moment and considered if she was holding the utensils in the best possible way. She was holding them in a jabbing manner and decided that a hammer grip might be more advantageous. Making the correction, she reached the landing and prepared to strike, only there was no immediate threat.

"Dammit, Ray, if you don't answer, I'm leaving your ass here."

But it was too late. Seneca had crossed the Rubicon. "Fuck it," she said.

She was all in now, and she was either going to die or live to tell one hell of a story. She hit the light switch and felt a heavy thump to the back of her head. Then everything went dark.

***

Rodney bent and lifted his quarry from the floor. She felt light as a feather as he set her in the chair in his mother's sewing room and unzipped her hoodie. Seneca's breasts seemed to pour from the unzipped hoodie, and Rodney averted his eyes. He'd been expecting her to be wearing a T-shirt. The sight of her pink bra suggested that he'd made the wrong selection yet again. With a feeling bordering on disgust, Rodney began preparing her for the test. He doubted she would pass; in fact, he was more certain than he had been with any of the others. Still, he had to try.

19

Chapter 19

Friday, May 10, 2019
Cedar Falls, Iowa

National Jones pulled into the parking lot of the Knights' Inn off Highway 58. Sabo had offered to let him crash at his place, but Jones opted for the motel. He figured it was probably cleaner and less likely to get raided by the DEA. Jones checked into Room 103, tossed his day bag onto the bed, kicked off his boots, and checked again to make sure the coffee stain hadn't set in. *Had that only happened this morning?* The spilled coffee, the ass-chewing by his boss, and the call out of the blue from Sabo. Oh, and let's not forget the news of the Tooth Fairy's return. And that was all before he left the office.

He supposed the biggest news of all, and like it

or not he had Sabo to thank for it, was that they finally had a picture of the killer. Had Sabo turned in the video like he was supposed to, who could say how long it would have been before the higher-ups decided to release the image to the press. Now the image would be all over the 5 O'clock News, and someone was sure as hell going to remember that face.

Jones massaged his temples, sat at the foot of his bed, and decided he would take a little catnap. There wasn't much he could do without Charlotte, and he hadn't had time to go over much of the case with her before she left for Tabor County to assist in; what was it, two dead cops? He checked his watch and grabbed the remote for the television. The local news was just starting, and sure as shit, the missing co-ed was the lead.

The anchor, a handsome young man with a granite chin, steel-blue eyes, and blinding white teeth, delivered the news. Just above his right shoulder, the producer floated a picture of Seneca. She looked much younger than she had in the video Jones had seen earlier, and he figured it might have been her high school graduation picture. Either way, a beautiful young blonde in danger was sure to get the viewers' attention. Then the news anchor dove into the deepest part of the sensationalism pool. "A source close to the investigation has informed this reporter that the authorities believe the young woman to be the latest victim of the Tooth Fairy, the prolific serial killer who has eluded police for more than a decade."

"Shit!"

Jones felt the fire rise up his neck and into his face. "Dammit! Sabo, you fucking idiot!" He got up and began pacing. "Why would he mention the fucking Tooth Fairy?" Jones began clenching and unclenching his jaw. If Sabo had been in the room with him, Jones doubted he could have kept from punching him in the face. He scratched at his bald head and chuffed out great exhalations in an effort to regain his composure so he could focus on the rest of the story. As he watched, Seneca's picture faded, and the grainy image of the guy believed to be the Tooth Fairy appeared on the screen. Jones had spent the last hour looking at the picture, but it still made him cringe.

"Authorities are asking for your assistance in identifying this man," the anchor said.

A pair of phone numbers scrolled across the bottom of the screen. They had to use their personal cell phone numbers. If any of the information turned out to be useful, he would have to act fast, but the reality was that most, if not all, would be complete bullshit. He grabbed a pen and notepad from his bag and sat down at the small table. The second the segment ended, his phone rang.

"Son of a bitch," he said to himself and then hit the accept button. "National—" he stopped himself. "Major Crimes, how can I help you?"

Call after call came through. Vigilantes called to offer their assistance in hunting the bastard down. Psychics called, and they did not disappoint. To their credit, each one said that they saw her body near water, and any cop who has ever worked a case with a psychic knew that "near water" was the go-to for the paranormal sect. Others called to offer condolences, but for the first hour, there was nothing useful. Then Jones got his first break.

The kid's name was Lucas Perez. He worked at a filling station in Waterloo, and he said that the suspect on the news had stopped in for gas yesterday morning. He said that he'd never seen him before but doubted that he'd ever forget him, what with all the scars and the missing eye.

"I never even would have seen him, but I was out loading the squeegee station with paper towels, and he looked right at me! I almost shit myself."

"About what time would you say this was?" Jones asked, ignoring the incoming calls and letting them go to voicemail.

"My shift ends at 9:00 AM. It was right before I got off."

"How did he pay?"

"Credit card at the pump, I guess. He never came inside."

"Is there a way to get a copy of that receipt?"

"Sure, we can pull it up."

"Great, and do you guys have surveillance video?"

"Yeah, but mostly it just points at the counter, you know, so the owner can make sure we aren't stealing."

"Do you have any that point toward the pumps?"

"Oh, yeah, we have a couple cameras out there."

"Are you working right now, Lucas?"

"No, I was actually just getting ready for bed. I like to try and get a few hours before I have to go in. I start at 1:00 AM."

"Well, I hate to do this, but can you give me the address of your gas station and meet me there?"

Jones could hear the caller exhale sharply. "I guess. You got something to write with?"

"Yep, go ahead."

Jones pulled his boots back on and adjusted his Stetson. He got in his car and tossed the notepad with the address on the seat next to him. Calls kept coming and interrupting his GPS, but he made good time to Chuck's Gas and Lube. He went in to ask for Lucas, and the man at the counter regarded Jones with a queer eye.

"What do you want with Lucas?"

"I'm a U.S. Marshal," Jones said. The response flowed naturally but unwanted from his lips.

The attendant looked at the Stetson on Jones's head. "Like Matt Dillon on *Gunsmoke*!"

"Yeah," Jones said, trying to hide his exasperation. "Just like that, only we don't ride horses anymore."

Jones was well aware that, even to this day, many of the marshals in the western territories rode almost daily as part of the job, but he didn't have the energy to go into it. "Lucas is going to help me with a case I'm working on. He's supposed to meet me here."

"Well, maybe I can help you. I'm Chuck, and this is my station."

"That sure would be great. Did you happen to catch the news?" he asked, nodding at the small television on the counter.

"No, been running in and out most of the day. Having trouble with the car wash," he said, jutting a thumb toward the small white brick building with CAR WASH $5.00 painted freehand in red paint on the side. "What can we do to help, Marshal?"

"Lucas said a man stopped for gas around 9:00 AM yesterday. Would you be able to pull the receipt?"

"Sure, if you can tell me which pump he used."

Jones looked out the window at the six gleaming

silver gas pumps reflecting the red of the setting sun. "Shit, I have no idea. What about video? Do you have video you can show me?"

Chuck walked over to the window and pointed up at the light pole. "Same problem. I have three cameras, one covering each of the sets of pumps. The monitor is pretty small, but I suppose you could see if you squint."

As they were talking, another customer walked in and asked for a pack of Chesterfields. "Scuse me a minute, would ya?"

"Of course," Jones answered.

While he waited, Jones walked over to the front window. The thought that the monster he'd spent over a decade searching for might have been right out there just a day ago sent a chill up his spine. He'd never been this close to him. Never had anything but bodies, taunting letters, and broken teeth to work with. The thought of finally being able to snap cuffs on his nemesis caused a slight twitch in his stomach, but it was short-lived. A young man in jeans and a gray button-down shirt that said Chuck's across the chest walked through the door.

"Hi, I'm Lucas. You must be the cop I spoke with on the phone," he said as he extended his hand.

Jones shook it. "National Jones, that's right. But how did you know who I was?"

"I dunno, you just look like a cop."

"Fair enough," Jones said with a slight smile. "Fair enough."

Chuck, who had finished with his customer, joined them. "I see you met Lucas."

"That I did. Now maybe we can get a few things nailed down."

"Sure, like what?" Lucas asked.

"Can you tell me what pump he used?" Jones asked.

"Yeah, that one," Lucas said and pointed. "Pump number 5, at the end."

"Excellent, and can you describe his car?"

"Yeah, old blue sedan, kind of a beater, ya know?"

"I'm on it," said Chuck, who hurried into the office.

"Did the guy say anything to you? Good morning, or — I don't know, anything?"

"No," Lucas said. "After we made eye contact, he turned his head away, like he didn't want me to look at him. I just figured it was because he was all messed up. His face, I mean."

"Do you think you could sit down with a forensic artist so they can work up a sketch?"

"I guess. I only saw him for a second, but like I said on the phone, I don't think I'll ever forget that face."

Chuck called from the office. "Hey, Marshal, you

got to see this."

Jones entered and sat in the chair next to Chuck's. The video was difficult to see. Spider webs had hung in the way of the camera, but there was no doubt. It was the same person from the laundry room surveillance video.

"That's him," Jones said firmly. "That's my guy."

"And here's the receipt for his transaction. He pumped seven gallons. The guy's name is—" Chuck ran a finger down the piece of paper and then stopped. "—here it is."

"Do you have an address?" Jones asked.

"Nope, you're gonna have to reach out to the credit card company for that."

Jones took the receipt. "Thank you both."

"Me and my people are always glad to help out the boys in blue," Chuck said.

"And we appreciate it. Now, if I could ask one more favor?"

"Shoot."

"Would you be able to make a copy of the video for me?"

As they spoke, another customer walked in, and Chuck nodded at Lucas. "Excuse me for a minute," Lucas said as he stepped away to assist.

"Said you need a copy of the video?"

"If it's not too much trouble."

"Shouldn't be," Chuck said as he flipped through a stack of discs. "DVD, okay?"

"Perfect," said Jones.

"Be just a minute," Chuck offered a salute with the shiny disc in his hand.

While he waited, Jones pulled his cell phone from his pocket. "Thirty-two missed calls. Holy shit." Jones shook his head and unlocked his cell as another call came in. Jones let it go to voicemail and placed a call to Sabo.

Sabo answered on the fourth ring. "Major Crimes, Detective Serradella, what do you got?"

"Who made you a detective?"

"Nation?"

"Yeah, listen. I need you to reach out to Charlotte."

He gave Sabo the name and the license plate number.

"Is that him? Is that our guy?"

"Could be. I don't think there are two guys that look like that."

"Holy crap, we got him. We fucking got him!"

"Maybe — maybe we got him. Let's not count our chickens, detective."

"Fuck you," Sabo laughed. "Nation, this is huge!"

Jones smiled. "Hell yeah, it is. But let's do our due diligence. No shortcuts, no screw-ups."

"Well, I hope you're right, then I can stop answering this fucking phone."

Jones had heard either his phone or Sabo's phone beep for incoming calls at least a half dozen times while they spoke. "Meet me at the Knights' Inn on Highway Fifty-Eight. We have work to do."

20

Chapter 20

Friday, May 10, 2019
Tabor County, Iowa

Billy Parks had taken shelter under a tree as the storms blew through during the night but still managed to get soaked. He'd been walking for a couple of hours, and his gym shoes squeaked and squished with each step. He could feel a blister forming on his right heel, and his stomach was letting him know that it was time to eat. He'd wandered pretty far from the main road after ditching his mom's Corolla, and there wasn't a damned thing around for miles. He unwrapped one of the sticks of gum he'd found in the glove compartment and shoved it in his mouth.

Billy had always been blessed with a particularly good sense of direction and knew that the main highway lay to the east. If he was going to survive, he would need to find food. And if he was going to find food, it would be somewhere on the main highway. So, with his sopping wet shoes on his sore feet, Billy turned east.

By noon, Billy had managed to make it back to the highway just north of the town of Meridian. He sat in the treeline behind a small mom-and-pop filling station called Ronson's Gas & Go. Billy maneuvered himself around to see the two gas pumps and noticed a sandwich board that read: *Good Food and Cold Beer*. He didn't have a dime to his name, but he had the gun, and that would do just as well.

He waited until the green Plymouth Neon pulled out of the lot and ran for the store. Billy decided that fast and hard was the best way to hit the place. He pushed the door open, and the jingling bell drew the attention of the attendant.

"Afternoon, son, what can I do—"

The big gun erupted, the attendant fell dead, and Billy felt the now-familiar rush through his body. In that instant, Billy forgot all about being hungry. He forgot all about being wet and all about the blister that had been biting his heel for the past two hours. Nothing existed in Billy's world except Billy. Billy and the rapturous pleasure he felt coursing hot through his veins. He could hear the thrumming of his heart as it drove the machinery that carried out his deepest desires, and that excited him all the more. But like all good things, this too had to come to an end. For Billy, the end was marked by the dinging of the Milton bell as a car pulled up to the pumps.

For the briefest of moments, Billy considered waiting to see if the driver came in and killing him too, but then he remembered his dwindling supply of bullets. He might need them in the coming days, so he dismissed the idea even though it would have pleased him deeply. After checking to make sure the driver wasn't heading straight in, Billy grabbed a plastic bag from behind the counter where the dead attendant lay and filled it with snacks and a few cans of cola. Carrying all he could, Billy took off through the back door and disappeared into the woods.

21

Chapter 21

Friday, May 10, 2019
Tabor County - Iowa

As soon as Charlotte Rittenhouse pulled off Highway 63, she could see activity up ahead. Several squad cars formed a roadblock barring unauthorized access to what she assumed would be the crime scene. There were a few dozen onlookers who milled about, craning their necks and whispering to one another, as well as several news vans parked with their satellite booms raised high in the air.

Charlotte pulled slowly through the crowd and held her badge out the window. One of the deputies charged with keeping the curious at bay quickly examined her credentials and waved her through. About a half-mile up the road, she came upon a line of squad cars and a van marked *Tabor County Coroner's Office*, but there was no one around. She exhaled and rubbed at the kink that had formed in her neck about ten miles outside the county line. She parked behind the last squad car and was just about to get out when her phone rang.

"Detective Rittenhouse," she answered

"Charlotte, it's Sabo."

"Hey," she said by way of a greeting. "Let me call you back, I just got here."

"Listen, we got a huge break in the case, and we need you to reach out to the D.O.T. and run a name and plate."

Charlotte grabbed her notepad and her pen. "Go ahead."

He gave her the plate and waited for her to jot it down.

"Okay, got it. What's the name?"

"Henry — I'll spell the last name for you." He spelled out Oehlerking one letter at a time. "Jones is pretty sure that's our guy."

"I'll get right on it," she said and hung up.

Sabo was right, it was a huge break and she needed to act on it right away. Her car didn't have a mobile data computer in it, and she didn't want to have to wait till she got back into her station, so she got out of her car and started checking the patrol vehicles. Cops were notorious for leaving their keys in their squads, and as luck would have it, the third car she tried paid off. She slid into the driver's seat and flipped up the monitor. She ran a soundex on the name and got only one Henry Oehlerking. According to the readout, Henry was born in 1923. She ran the numbers in her head.

"That can't be the same guy. That would make him ninety-six years old."

She punched in the plate number and waited for the information to pop up. The screen flashed just as the door to the squad car flew open and Charlotte was pulled from the driver's seat by a strong hand that slammed her up against the car.

"What the hell do you think you're doing?" the deputy pinned her to the car, ran his free hand down her side and felt the gun on her hip. "Don't fucking move."

"I'm detective Charlotte Rittenhouse, Northeast Major Crimes."

"I don't give a fuck who you are," he said. "Do not move."

Charlotte nodded and did as she was told. The deputy keyed his mic. "Cantore, get over to your squad, now."

"My ID is in my back pocket," Charlotte said as calmly as she could. "My badge is on my belt right by my gun."

"I told you to shut up!"

Charlotte had had enough of the manhandling. "No, you told me not to move, and I told you that I'm a detective with Major Crimes, so unless you want a write-up, I suggest you get the fuck off of me."

The deputy didn't seem impressed and kept her pinned until his back-up arrived. Deputy Cantore came running out of the woods and cleared his gun from his holster.

"Anderson, what do ya got?" he asked excitedly.

"Put your fucking gun away, and just stand here while I pat her down," Anderson said.

He reached into her back pocket and pulled out her wallet. He flipped it open, though he probably really didn't need to. Any cop knew the feel of a wallet with a badge in it. He released his hold and Charlotte spun around, red in the face.

"What the fuck?" Charlotte demanded as she straightened her jacket. "Is this how you treat all assisting agencies?"

"Sure is, if I catch them breaking into my car."

"I didn't break in. You left it unlocked with the keys in it."

Anderson shot Cantore a look and Charlotte immediately recognized the relationship. "Let me guess, you're the FTO?"

Anderson exhaled sharply. "Deputy Jeff Anderson," he said, and offered his hand. "No hard feelings?"

Charlotte shook his hand. "You need to keep this one on a shorter leash."

"But you still haven't told me what you were doing in my car."

"Yeah, I'm sorry about that. I'm working this other case. My team is hunting a serial killer and I just got a big break — well, I thought it was a break anyway."

"And?"

"I had to run a plate."

"You know that's a LEADS violation, right?" Cantore sneered.

"So is leaving your terminal open for anyone to access," she fired back.

"Fair enough," Anderson said, throwing his hands up. "So, are you here to help with my dead deputy or work your other case?"

Disappointed in her discovery, Charlotte raised a hand in acquiescence. "I guess I'm all yours."

"Glad to hear it," Anderson said. "Let's head over to the scene. The ETs are working it, but you can at least get a feel for things."

***

Sabo knocked on the door to Room 103 and let himself in. Jones, who was still pissed, was sitting at the table watching the breaking news report from Tabor County and signaled for Sabo to be quiet.

216

The young reporter on the screen — who, to Jones, looked remarkably like the prototype for the Barbie Doll, stood with her hand to her ear waiting for the hand-off.

"And here with that story is our own investigative journalist, Jennifer Underback."

"Thank you, Chad," Jennifer began. "From our vantage point, it's very hard to see, but sources tell me that two bodies have been recovered from the wooded area directly behind me."

The cameraman panned off Jennifer and drew a tighter shot of a walking path that welcomed hikers to Dunn's Hollow.

"According to my source, the body of a sheriff's deputy along with the body of a young man believed to be a high school student were discovered early this morning by police. All of this stemming from a shooting which has sent another sheriff's deputy to Shining Cross Hospital in critical condition."

The cameraman panned back to Jennifer and closed in tight on her as she continued. "Late last night, law enforcement responded to the area and were fired upon by a suspect who then fled. With me is a neighbor who heard the shots and witnessed the escape."

The camera panned wide, and a man wearing a blue work shirt and a ball cap came into view. A caption appeared at the bottom of the screen that read, *Leo Henderson, neighbor.*

"Mr. Henderson, thank you for speaking with us."

"My pleasure."

"Can you tell our viewers what you saw?"

"Yeah, I can. The boy who lives in that house over there, the older one, not the younger one. The younger one's okay, but the older one..." Mr. Henderson shook his head. "I know you said I can't say his name, but everyone around here knows who he is, and they know he's a hellion like his old man."

Jennifer smiled nervously. "Yes, and can you tell us what you saw last night?"

"Like I was saying, I heard three gunshots, big ones. I'm guessing it was a forty-five. Anyway, I hear the shots and run out to my porch. I see a police car out there, no lights on or nothing, but it was parked under that streetlight there," he said, and pointed. "Then I look toward the Par—"

"No, no, we aren't using names, Mr. Henderson."

"Right, sorry. I look over at that house there, and I see the deputy laying at the bottom of the stairs, and then I see the older boy bolt out of the house and jump in his momma's Corolla and tear out. Then more police came and the ambulance and — well, it didn't look too good for the deputy."

"Thank you, Mr. Henderson," Jennifer said as

the camera tightened back onto her face. "My source tells me that the bodies in the woods are not related to the shooting. As many of you may recall, Dunn's Hollow was the site of another tragedy. In 2014, the body of Richie Barrett, eight years old, was discovered in these same woods. A local hunter made the gruesome discovery and reported it to the police. No arrest was made in the Richie Barrett slaying, leading some to question whether or not the killer may have returned to his hunting ground. More as this story unfolds. I'm Jennifer Underback, reporting live for Channel 17 News."

"What the fuck was that?"

"That," said Jones, "is what Charlotte got called away on."

22

Chapter 22

Friday, May 10, 2019
Tabor County – Iowa

With his need for food satiated, and his appetite for violence newly aroused, Billy hiked deeper into the countryside and away from prying eyes. The midday sun burned high in the sky, so he did his best to keep to the treeline. When he'd stopped to eat, Billy took off everything but his underwear and laid it all down in the tall grass to dry. While he ate and waited for the hot sun to suck the moisture out of his blue jeans, Billy fiddled a bit with the revolver. He knew enough to keep his finger out of the trigger guard and managed to find the cylinder release. After removing the spent casings, Billy discovered that he had only one bullet left. He felt especially smart for not wasting it on the guy who stopped for gas.

He pitched the empty shell casings, dropped the live round back into the cylinder, and snapped it shut. Then he got dressed and continued on. He didn't know exactly where he was going, but southwest felt right.

* * *

They'd only gone a few feet when FTO Anderson must have noticed Deputy Cantore following. Anderson stopped, and Charlotte almost walked right into him. He shook his head and turned toward Cantore.

"Seriously?"

Cantore looked dumbfounded. "What?"

"Lock the squad," he said, sounding more like an impatient father than a training officer.

Charlotte snickered under her breath but felt a little bad for the young deputy. She'd had her share of ass-chewings as a recruit, and they had always left her feeling stupid and incompetent. She promised herself that she would never treat a new officer that way if she ever became a field training officer, but that promise lasted three weeks into training her second recruit, and shit like this was why.

Cantore hurried back to the squad and was about

221

to lock it up when he saw the image on the screen. "Who's Rodney Oehlerking?" he asked. "Is that your guy?"

"That says Henry, not Rodney," she said, sharing a look with Anderson.

"I can read," Cantore called back. "This says Rodney Oehlerking."

"What? Let me see," she said, hurrying back.

Cantore stepped aside and pointed at the screen. "See for yourself," he said smugly.

Charlotte immediately checked the date of birth. This guy was born in 1952. Again, she did the math in her head. "Sixty-seven, yeah, that's totally possible."

"What's going on?" Anderson asked.

Charlotte scrolled down the readout. It said that Rodney Oehlerking was 6'6" tall and weighed 187 pounds. "Holy shit. I gotta get to a D.O.T. site. I need to get a copy of this guy's license."

"What are you talking about?" Anderson asked. "I thought you were here to help with our case."

"I am, but I need to get this information to my team. And first I need to see what this guy looks like. I need to make sure I'm right."

Anderson huffed and shook his head. "Un-fucking believable. The one and only time I call for assistance from you guys and my case goes on the back burner."

"Boss," said Cantore, "she's hunting a serial killer. With all due respect—," he lowered his eyes momentarily, "—Lawson's gone, and we know the kid shot Deputy Rollins."

Anderson's neck was bright red, and the color was creeping up his face.

"Besides, she can do both," Cantore continued.

"What?" Charlotte asked. "How can I do both?"

"Well, you can pull up the image from his license right here," Cantore said. "Can I—"

Charlotte hopped out of the car, and Cantore slid in. Anderson stepped in behind Charlotte and watched over her shoulder as Cantore's fingers flew over the keyboard. A second later, the computer blipped, and the image popped up. Charlotte's hand flew to her mouth.

"What the hell is that?" Anderson asked indelicately.

"That," Charlotte answered, "is the Tooth Fairy."

Cantore laughed, obviously never having heard of the prolific killer. Anderson just stared at the screen.

"You've got to be shitting me."

"No, I'm not," Charlotte said.

She filled them in on the video from the laundry room and the most recent victim, Seneca Campbell. Then she excused herself and placed a call to Sabo.

There was no answer, and the call went to voicemail. The cheery voice announced that the mailbox was full and offered an even cheerier "Goodbye!" She tried a few more times, but each time the results were the same, then opted to send a text. The message was simple and to the point. *Get down here now!* She shared her location and met back up with Cantore and Anderson, the latter standing with his arms crossed, glaring impatiently.

"I'm sorry, Deputy Anderson, it's just—"

"Save it!" he snapped.

"Look, I really want to help with your case, and I will. I just need to get ahold of my partners."

"And how did that work out for you?"

"They didn't answer," she said, sounding deflated. "So, I sent them a text."

"You think maybe I can borrow you for a few minutes while you await their reply?"

"Absolutely! What can I do to help?"

Anderson was still red in the face. "Seeing as I have no idea how long I'll have you; I'll have you start by canvassing the crowd."

Charlotte got the message loud and clear. She had pissed Anderson off, and he was punishing her with grunt work. But Charlotte Rittenhouse hadn't gotten to where she was by letting people shit on her. "Look, no offense, but that's a job for the rookie," she said, jutting a thumb at Cantore.

"Oh, don't worry. He'll be helping you," Anderson said.

Cantore didn't even bat an eye. He was used to shit details. The young recruit reached into his duty bag, grabbed a clipboard, and hopped out of the car. "Ready when you are."

"Deputy Anderson, you can't be serious."

"Detective Rittenhouse, I am dead serious. Now, please excuse me. I have to get back to *my* crime scene."

He left Charlotte with her jaw hanging open and then turned back toward the car. Charlotte smirked; she knew he was bluffing. There was no way anyone with half a brain would waste the skills of a Major Crimes detective on a wild goose chase.

"Change your mind?" she asked smugly.

"No, I forgot the bug spray."

Charlotte stood, hands on hips, and squared up to the much larger deputy. "I didn't drive two hours to help with a fucking canvass. Get some of your deputies to bang on doors. Now, either you want my help, or you can explain to your boss how you wasted my time on bullshit work."

Anderson seemed unfazed by her tirade. "I don't know what kind of Skynet-Cyberdyne bullshit you Major Crimes geniuses use to solve your cases, but out here, we use good old-fashioned legwork. Now, either you get with the program, or you jump back in that—" He looked at Bernie's rusted quarter panels and balding tires. "—pile of shit and head back to the city."

Charlotte was about to blow her top when she pictured Tom Parnell's face and imagined his squeaky, pimply voice chewing her a new asshole. "Fine, I'll play it your way."

"Good."

He said it without the slightest satisfaction, and that just pissed Charlotte off all the more. Like it was a foregone conclusion that she would fall into line. Then, without missing a beat, she said, "Just one question."

"Shoot," Anderson replied.

"What the hell are Skynet and Cyberdyne?"

He looked at her. "You've got to be kidding. You haven't seen the Terminator?"

"The movie from the eighties?" she asked, doing her best to sound incredulous.

"Yeah, that one."

"That movie came out like ten years before I was born, she fudged a little on her age. I think it's time for you to see some new movies."

Anderson shook his head and turned for the woods. Cantore stared wide-eyed at Anderson. "I have never seen anyone talk to Deputy Anderson like that." Then in a whisper he said, "You're my hero."

Charlotte glanced down at her phone, only half-listening to Cantore. "Thanks. I actually watched all those movies with my father. He was a huge sci-fi guy."

"Still, it was pretty cool."

Charlotte smiled. "Is he always so pleasant?"

"No," Cantore said. "FTO Anderson is a really good guy. It's just that we're super short-handed. We had to send a bunch of our guys down near Meridian. There was a robbery at a gas station, and I guess the clerk got shot."

Charlotte felt like an ass, but what was done was done. "Well, then let's get started," she said. "Come on, I'll drive."

They pulled up to the roadblock and parked. The crowd had grown since she had arrived, and it seemed more were coming by the minute. Charlotte assumed that was because of all the sensationalist news stories. As they walked among the crowd, Charlotte did her best to separate the possible witnesses from the regular looky-loos. Before gathering any information, she asked each person where they lived. If they didn't live in the immediate area, she gave them to Cantore.

As Charlotte milled through the crowd, she came upon a beautiful, statuesque blonde who looked entirely out-of-place standing on a dirt road in the middle of rural Iowa. The woman was interviewing a young boy on his bicycle and a woman who appeared to be his mother. Charlotte caught the tail end of the interview.

"How tall would you say the man was?" Jennifer Underback, investigative reporter, asked the boy.

"Real tall, way taller than you," he said innocently. "And he had a bump on his back and a big apple in his throat."

"Apple?" Jennifer asked.

"He means Adam's apple, ma'am?" the mother answered.

"Yeah, and he drove a junky blue car, and he was peeing in the woods!" The boy suddenly looked nervous. "I wasn't supposed to tell that part."

"Did you speak with the man?" Charlotte asked, sounding surprised.

"Yeah, he said that I shouldn't tell my mom that he was peeing in the woods."

"What?" the mother asked. "Did he touch you?"

"No, but—" He paused like he was searching for the right words. "I know it's not nice to say, but his face was all messed up!"

Charlotte stepped between the boy and the reporter and began speaking with him and his mother. The cameraman moved to the side and set the frame so that he could capture the interaction. Charlotte placed a hand over the lens and pushed it aside.

"Excuse me," Jennifer said. "Just who do you—"

Charlotte produced her badge, and Jennifer stepped aside. The camera followed her, and she carried on like a pro. "It seems that we have just broken some important news here, ladies and gentlemen. I'll dig a little more and check back in, Chad. Reporting live for Channel 17 News, I'm Jennifer Underback," she said and gave her cameraman the *cut* sign.

"What else can you tell me about this man?" Charlotte asked the little boy as she pulled away from the reporter.

"And who are you?" asked his mother.

"I'm Detective Rittenhouse, Major Crimes. Would you mind coming with me?"

"Where to?" asked the boy's mother.

Charlotte nodded. "Just the other side of the roadblock, so we can talk more privately."

"Hey, not so fast," Jennifer said, stepping back toward them. "This is my story."

"It's not a story, it's an active investigation," Charlotte fired back.

Jennifer backed down immediately. She knew that those words, *active investigation,* meant that she could be barred from speaking with the boy, and that was where the story was taking her.

"I'm sorry," she said, smiling her brightest smile. "But I did find the boy. Can you just give me a little something that I can use?"

Charlotte thought she sounded desperate, like a junkie just wanting a little taste. "I'll tell you what, if there is anything that I think your reporting might do to help the case, you'll be the first one I go to."

"Fair enough," Jennifer said with a sharp nod.

The little boy, Ben, told Charlotte and Cantore everything he had seen. He even described the deformities on the man's face. Charlotte cursed herself for not letting Cantore drive. She wanted desperately to show the boy the image on his computer screen.

"Cantore, would you mind taking my car back and bringing your car up? I want to show Ben the picture."

"We aren't supposed to let civilians see the MDCs."

Charlotte looked at Cantore, and he understood immediately. This was not the time to question her. But he offered a helpful suggestion instead.

"I can show it to him on my phone if you want."

"What are you talking about?"

"I sent a copy of the image to my phone. I figured we might need it."

If not for the timing, Charlotte might have kissed the young deputy right on the lips. "Don't just stand there; let's see it."

Cantore pulled up the image and handed his

phone to her. She then showed the image to Ben's mother. "Would it be okay if he looked at this?"

The mother hitched in a breath. "Oh my God."

"I know, so what do you say?"

"If it will help, I guess it will be alright. Are you sure you want to see this, Benjie?"

"Yeah, Mom, and please stop calling me that!"

Charlotte braced herself and turned the image toward the little boy.

"Yep," Ben said calmly. "That's him."

Charlotte felt a shiver run up her spine and clear down to her fingertips. She leaned against the car's rear bumper. "We're going to need some information."

The words came out even though she didn't realize she was speaking. And Cantore must have sensed it. He gathered contact information on the boy and his mother and pulled his business card from his pocket.

"I'm going to jot Detective Rittenhouse's name on the back of my card. Ben, buddy, if you remember anything else, you guys can call me and I'll get a message to the detective."

Ben nodded, and his mother took the card. After making sure they didn't have any questions, Cantore instructed Ben and his mother not to speak with anyone regarding what they had just seen. "And anyone includes the nice reporter lady, right?"

"Yep," Ben said and flashed a thumbs up. Then his face dropped. "Is he a really bad man?"

"He sure is, kid," Cantore said.

"Does he know where I live?"

Charlotte watched as Cantore knelt down in front of Ben and placed a hand on his shoulder. "Nope, and we sure aren't going to let him find out."

Ben smiled, but his mother still looked worried.

"I'll see if we can have a squad make a couple of passes by your place for the next few weeks. How does that sound?"

That seemed to ease her mind, and Cantore escorted them back out past the roadblock.

"Thanks," Charlotte said.

Cantore smiled and sat next to her on the bumper. "I guess FTO Anderson was right about the *good old-fashioned police work*."

Charlotte smiled back. "I guess he was."

Cantore slapped his thighs and got up. "When you're ready, I'll take you over to meet Detective Sullivan. He's the detective in charge."

"No time like the present." Just then, her phone rang. "Rittenhouse."

"Charlotte, it's Sabo."

"Where the hell have you guys been?"

"Look, we got a big break—"

"Well, get your asses down here. I need you

guys!”

23

Chapter 23

Friday, May 10, 2019
Oehlerking Farm – Rural Iowa

S eneca woke to the sensation of something tugging on her head, followed by an explosion of pain and the hard snap of her tooth cracking. The crack came as a thud that she felt from her head down into the pit of her stomach. She could taste the blood running down the back of her throat and immediately probed the gap with her tongue. She touched an exposed nerve, and the pain blossomed again. As it faded to an agonizing throb, Seneca became aware of the aching at the back of her head. Her first thought was that she must have been in an accident, but the pain was sobering. Slowly, very slowly, her world came into focus.

Blinking with the throbs, she took a moment to

gather her senses. There was a pungent, musty smell that reminded her of her grandmother's root cellar, and the air felt heavy and uncomfortably hot. She tried to swallow but gagged on the blood that flooded her mouth, and then, finally, her vision began to clear. The first thing she noticed was the clear plastic gown that covered her from the neck down. It was the kind of thing her mother would make her wear when she cut her hair.

Beneath the plastic, Seneca could see the curve of the tops of her breasts. She'd been wearing a hoodie, but that was gone. Great globs of blood that had fallen from her mouth spattered the transparent gown, and she became aware of a sharp pain in her shoulders. She tried to move and realized that her hands were tied behind her back. With each jerking movement, what felt like shards of glass ricocheted through her brain. Bright flashes of pain erupted behind her eyes.

"What the fuck is going on?" she mumbled, the "F" lost to her missing tooth.

"No! Mother doesn't like that kind of language," Rodney said as he slid two large catch basins beneath her feet and then rose to his full height. "Hopefully, we won't be needing these."

Her hearing was the last of her senses to return. She felt clammy saliva hit her face and smelled rancid breath, but the voice was muffled, like she had some kind of membrane stretched over her ears. When she saw his face, the shrillness of her scream tore through.

Rodney grabbed her face and dug his fingers into her cheeks to force her mouth open. She tried to fight. She pinched her lips shut and tried to move her head, but he had her and he wasn't letting go. He worked a finger between her lips and into the small gap formed by the missing tooth. He pressed on the nerve, and Seneca's mouth flew open, then he jammed the wooden handle of his hatchet between her jaws. He used the handle to control her head as he reached for the nail puller.

Seneca remembered her grandparents' horse farm back in Omaha. As a child, she used to watch her grandfather pull horseshoe nails with the same tool, only this one looked sharp and dripped red with her blood. The tool moved closer and closer in Rodney's gnarled hands.

24

Chapter 24

Friday, May 10, 2019
Tabor County, Iowa

J ones's Volkswagen Atlas gobbled up the road, and in an hour and a half, they were turning onto Avenue J. He and Sabo made for Burns Court and stopped in front of a very serious but very young-looking deputy. The deputy held his hand up, ordering Jones to stop, and Jones obliged.

"Afternoon, Deputy," he said as he reached into his back pocket and fished for his ID.

The deputy tensed, and his hand moved slowly toward his belt in a gesture of classical conditioning that would have made Pavlov proud. Jones assumed that had he been driving his department-issued Ford Explorer with its government plates, the deputy would have responded differently —

or at least he hoped that would have been the case. Either way, as soon as Jones produced his U.S. Marshals' badge, the young man loosened up.

"Afternoon, Marshal. What can I do for you?"

"We're here to see Detective Rittenhouse."

"She's inside, but I can't let you go in there. It's still a crime scene. We're just waiting for the ETs… um, I mean evidence technicians."

"Yes," said Jones. "I know what ETs are."

"Right, sorry. Anyway, they're finishing up with the bodies in the woods. When they're done, they have to process this scene. I can't let you in."

"That's fine," Jones said. "But do you think you could let Detective Rittenhouse know we're here?"

"I would, sir, but I can't leave my post."

He didn't mean to, but Jones rolled his eyes, a careless gesture that would only serve to demean the young deputy. He'd always done his best to make the people he came in contact with feel valued. It was a lesson his mother taught him, but some-times he missed the mark. Quickly, Jones redirected the target of his eye roll.

"Of course, you can't. It was stupid of me to ask," he said. "I'll just try her cell phone. Is it okay if I park here?"

The deputy shifted on his feet and looked around. "I'll tell you what. You're a cop, right?"

Jones smiled. "Yeah, something like that."

The deputy looked around again. "Can you just hang here a minute? I'll go get her for you. Just please," he held up pleading hands, "don't let anyone in or it'll be my ass."

Jones tapped the brim of his Stetson. "You have my word as a member of the oldest law enforcement agency in the country."

"The what?"

Jones shook his head. "Never mind," and held up an apologetic hand. And with that, the deputy turned and sprinted for the house.

Jones and Sabo got out and leaned against the Volkswagen's hood. Jones breathed in the hot air and listened to the cicadas buzzing madly in the trees. They weren't out of the air-conditioned car for two minutes before beads of sweat formed on their foreheads. Sabo swiped at the moisture.

"Poor fucking kid. He has to stand out here all day, and it's as hot as a pair of balls in flannel underwear."

Jones pulled a handkerchief from his pocket and dabbed his forehead. "Well, I can't say I know what that feels like, but I'm sure you're not far off."

He folded his handkerchief and tucked it back into his pocket just as another deputy came walking up. This deputy was older than the kid. He had hard-set eyes and the face of a man in charge. He walked straight up to Jones, and without batting an eye, demanded an explanation.

"Who are you, and why are you in my crime scene?"

Jones extended a hand. "US Marshal, National Jones," he said and read the deputy's name tag. "And I believe I am just outside *your* crime scene, Deputy Anderson."

Anderson reached forward and shook his hand. "Sorry, this place is crawling with fucking reporters." He looked at Jones's Stetson. "Shoulda figured you for a marshal," he said with a smirk.

Jones knew right away that he liked this guy and offered a genuine smile. "I'm—" he started and then corrected himself, "—we're here to assist Detective Rittenhouse."

Anderson leaned in close to Jones's ear just as Charlotte came out from the side door of the Parks' house. "She's a hard charger, that one."

Jones smiled again. "That she is."

Charlotte gave Anderson a look that wasn't lost on Jones. "You guys made great time."

"It's a good thing all the deputies in Tabor County are busy," Sabo said.

This time the eye roll was aimed and deliberate.

"What? I just meant... you know, you were speed-ing."

"So, what have we got?" Jones asked Charlotte, disregarding Sabo's obtuse comment.

"Me and Sully... that's Detective Sullivan, we have to head down to Meridian. It looks like the kid that shot Deputy Rollins may have pulled a robbery at a gas station there and killed the clerk."

"You said there were two deputies shot," Jones said.

"The one here," she said, and nodded toward the blood-stained ground just outside the front door, "he was shot. We think Deputy Lawson, whose body was found in the woods, was killed by Oehlerking."

Jones's face fell in on itself. "You think the Tooth Fairy was here?"

"Yes, we think Rodney is his name. The name you provided," she flipped through her notepad, "Henry Oehlerking, was probably his father. If he's alive, he's in his nineties. Definitely not our guy."

Jones was still trying to get his head around the fact that he was getting closer to his quarry.

"Anyway, we think maybe Rodney stopped to take a piss, and Deputy Lawson rolled up on him. Somehow, Deputy Lawson's body ended up about 800 yards into the woods. We're still trying to piece it all together, but it looks like Billy Parks... that's the one that shot Rollins, and his little brother Joey came upon Deputy Lawson, and Billy took his gun. There was no sign of Seneca, but we found another body in the woods near Deputy Lawson's." Again, Charlotte referred to her notepad. "A male white believed to be in his mid to late teens, probably a high school student. He had a large amount of cannabis in his pockets, all bagged up for sale. The cause of death appears to be a large-caliber bullet wound to the neck. Our suspect's brother, Joey Parks, said that he was with Billy when Billy shot the unidentified subject. He didn't have a wallet or identification on him, but we know it's not Oehlerking."

"And why do you think the kid is responsible for the gas station attendant?"

"After he shot Deputy Rollins, Billy Parks took off in his mother's car. The car was discovered abandoned and out of gas. Sully sent a K-9 out to the scene, and the dog followed the scent to the gas station."

Jones took a deep breath. The expression, like trying to drink from a firehose, popped into his head. "That's a lot to take in," he said.

"I know," Charlotte said. "It *is* a lot to take in. What I need from you and Sabo is to track down an address for this guy. His DL shows a PO box over in Montour, so we figure he lives out that way somewhere."

"Where the hell is Montour?" Jones asked.

"Just outside the western border of Tabor County," said a man sporting a handgun and badge on his hip. He wore blue jeans and a gray button-down shirt and looked nothing like a cop in Jones's estimation. "Hi, I'm Sully."

Jones met his handshake. "National Jones, US Marshal."

"No shit! Hey, I heard about you." He was all smiles. "Dude, that hat."

"That's a Stetson, you hipster dipshit," Anderson said.

"Nice Stetson. Man, I could never pull that off."

"Not without a haircut," Anderson said with a smile.

"Don't mind Jeff," Sully said. "He's a salty old bastard."

"We should get going," Charlotte interrupted.

"You should ride with me," Sully suggested.

"Good idea," Charlotte said.

Jones noticed the slight awkwardness in the exchange but didn't mention it. "Okay, and we'll head toward Montour and see what we can find out."

With that, they all retreated to their cars and drove off. Jones and Sabo hopped in the Volkswagen and followed Charlotte and Sully as they headed west for Montour.

"What the hell was that with Charlotte and that guy?" Sabo asked.

"I don't know," said Jones. "I wondered the same thing. She's wearing a wedding band."

"Yeah, but her husband is a piece of shit. He's

probably banging some flight attendant as we speak."

"He's a pilot?" Jones asked.

"No, Alex is a flight attendant, but there are a lot of *layovers,* if you know what I mean."

"That doesn't mean he's screwing around, and even if he is, that doesn't mean she can —you know what, that's none of our business," Jones said, trying to stop the gossip.

"Me and Charlotte go way back, and I know she's given him a lot of chances. I've spent hours with her at St. Elmo's listening to her cry in her beer. She's a great girl, Nation, and she deserves a good guy."

"It's not as easy as that when you're married. It's not like switching cell phone carriers."

"Well, whatever," Sabo said. "She just deserves a good guy, not another smooth prick like this Sully guy."

Jones shook his head. "And how do you know this *Sully guy* is a smooth prick?"

"I know because he's just like me," Sabo said.

They drove the rest of the way to Montour in silence.

25

Chapter 25

Friday, May 10, 2019
Meridian, Iowa

The parking lot for Ronson's Gas & Go was wrapped in yellow police tape, but the deputy standing guard lifted the tape and motioned Sully's unmarked car into the lot. He parked next to one of the squads to make sure he didn't drive over anything important and he and Charlotte exited the cool car for the heat of the day. Charlotte shielded her eyes from the glare and felt beads of sweat forming on her lip.

"Why the hell is it so hot? It's only May."

Sully shrugged his shoulders. "I don't know, global warming?"

"You're not serious, right?" Charlotte asked.

Sully shrugged again.

"Cause that is not how global warming works. You know that, right?"

"Look, college girl," he said with a smile, "all I know about the weather is I wear a jacket when it's cold, I carry an umbrella when it rains, and when it's hot as hell, I bitch and moan until I get back in the AC."

"Touché."

"Maybe when all this is over, you can buy me a drink and tell me all about climate change and greenhouse gasses."

The smile fell from her face and Sully must have noticed. "Hey, that's not a come on or anything. I know you're married." He pointed at her ring then flashed a coy smile. "I just like free booze."

The guy was handsome, there was no doubt about that, and if she were single — hell, if she were even separated, she would absolutely try and get him drunk. But Charlotte was neither of those things. No, she was her daddy's daughter, John Rittenhouse had spent thirty-two years on the job and had never had his integrity questioned. He taught her that all they had as police officers was their integrity. That they owed it to the badge and to the people that they served to live an untarnished life.

"No, of course," Charlotte said diplomatically. "I knew what you meant, and I would love for the four of us to grab a beer when this is over. Believe me, if we catch the Tooth Fairy, Nation will be buying rounds of champagne."

Now it was Sully's smile that faded a bit. "Is he a good guy?"

"Who, Nation?"

"Yeah, is he... you know, a good dude?"

"I don't really know him. I only met him earlier today, but Sabo really likes him, and even though Sabo is a bit of a goof, he wouldn't have called him in on this if he wasn't solid."

"That's good," Sully said as they approached the front door to the station. "I hope the AC is on in there."

A monster of a German Shepherd lay on the floor pressed up against a bag of ice. He raised his head when Charlotte entered but quickly lost interest and placed his head back on the cool floor. Its leash was connected to a deputy wearing BDUs and bouncing the heels of his black boots off the side of the cooler he was sitting on.

"You two the detectives we've been waiting for?"

"I'm Detective Rittenhouse, Northeast Major Crimes."

"Major Crimes for a simple robbery-gone-wrong?"

"It's more than that."

The deputy turned to Sully. "Hey, Sully, how's it

hanging?"

"Charlotte, this is Deputy Stuart Little."

Charlotte couldn't stifle the laugh, though she tried covering her mouth. Deputy Little just shook his head.

"I know, I've heard them all. My personal favorite being the classic; what are you, a man or a mouse?"

"I'm sorry," Charlotte said and held a hand up in apology. "Nice to meet you, Stuart. What's your partner's name?"

"This one-hundred-and-twenty-pound furry chainsaw is Apex. Best tracker and take-down specialist in the Hawkeye State. And you can call me Stu."

"Were you guys first on scene?"

Stu pointed. "She was."

An officer in a Meridian P.D. uniform came out of the back room wearing rubber gloves and carrying a camera. She wore her hair in a tight ponytail and had an oppressive scowl on her face.

"I thought I heard the bell ring."

Charlotte looked above her head at the small brass bell mounted above the door. "Hi, I'm Charlotte Rittenhouse. One of the detectives assigned to this case. This is my partner — um." She realized she 'd forgotten his name. "Sully," she said, finally.

"Sullivan, Detective Kevin Sullivan, but everyone

calls me Sully, even my partner," he said, offering a disarming smile.

"I'm officer Erica Morales, and this is my scene."

Stu shrugged. "I sure as hell don't want it."

"That's good, cause you ain't getting it. I told him to sit his ass on that cooler and not to move."

Stu threw his hands up. "I ain't moving, baby."

Sully looked confused, but Charlotte understood. Police work was a boy's club, and she knew all too well how hard it was for a woman to make her mark. "Of course, Officer Morales, we're only here to help."

That was bullshit, and every cop in that place knew it, Morales included. Once Major Crimes showed up, it was their show, but she seemed to appreciate the gesture and began sharing what she knew with the detectives.

"It looks like our shooter entered through the side door." She pointed to a glass door with dusting powder smeared all over it. "Then he approached the counter." Morales walked to the counter and raised her finger like a gun. "And shot the clerk."

The clerk's body still lay on the ground where he fell. Charlotte wasn't surprised. She knew the body couldn't be removed until the coroner came for it, and coroners always took their sweet-ass time arriving on scene. The clerk's shirt was open and small EKG tabs were stuck all over his body.

Morales must have noticed Charlotte looking at them and answered her question before she asked it.

"He was dead when I got here, but the fucking evidence eradication team had to do their thing. You know how they like stickers."

Charlotte had been surprised by a dead body once before, so she didn't begrudge the medics doing *their thing*. It happened one night during a midnight shift. She came across what she thought was a dead deer on Little Hawk Road, a two-lane that ran through a heavily wooded area that was notorious for roadkill. Charlotte hit her overheads, pulled onto the shoulder, and got out. She pulled on her gloves and walked over to the mangled thing, intending to drag it out of the roadway.

The boy, who looked to be about fifteen years old, lay on his back staring dead-eyed up into the night sky. His bicycle lay in the ditch about twenty feet away, suggesting to Charlotte that he'd been dragged, and his torn clothing seemed to bear that out. She called it in as a fatal hit-and-run, lit some flares, and waited for the cavalry to arrive. When the paramedics showed up, they ripped the boy's shirt open and ran leads to his chest. *Why bother?* she thought to herself, but sure as shit, the monitor blipped, and the medics went to work. The boy had suffered a traumatic brain injury but lived long enough for his family to be there when he passed. It wasn't much, but it was closure.

"They have no idea how badly they screw up our crime scenes," Sully said.

"Either that, or they don't give a shit," Morales added.

"They have their job and we have ours," Charlotte said, and switched topics. "What about surveillance video?"

"In this place?" Morales said. "Just look around, I'm surprised they have indoor plumbing."

The station had a certain early American Mayberry charm about it. White tile walls, black and white checkered floors. The cash register was an old non-electric lever-button-job, and the pop machine looked like something stolen from the set of the old TV show.

"Kind of quaint," Charlotte said. "But yeah, I get your point."

"Well, when you're done farting around in here, Apex is ready to go again," Stu said, hopping off the cooler.

26

Chapter 26

Friday, May 10, 2019
Montour, Iowa

J ones parked in front of the Montour Post Office and he and Sabo got out. The heat fell on them like a blanket. They hurried up the stairs and entered the eerie silence of the post office. The place smelled much as one would expect from an old postal facility. Jones stepped past the first person in line, flashed his U.S. Marshal's badge at the teller, and demanded to see the Postmaster. The teller wasn't impressed.

"Wait over by the closed window and I'll see what I can do."

Jones locked his eyes on the thin, pale postal worker and didn't budge. "I'll tell you what you're going to do, you're going to walk back there," he pointed at the wall behind the young man, "and get the Postmaster up here now! If you don't, you'll be leaving here in handcuffs for impeding a federal agent's investigation. Are we clear?"

Without another word, the young man sprinted for the backroom and did not return. Instead, a heavyset woman with impossibly black hair came storming to the front and slammed her meaty fists into her meaty hips.

"What in the world is going on up here and why is my teller crying?"

"Afternoon, ma'am, I'm U.S. Marshal National Jones, and this is a matter of life and death."

The woman seemed far more impressed than her teller had. "Well, let's just see what we can do to help." With that, she promptly buzzed Jones and Sabo into the inner office. "Philip, you get it to-gether and get back up here! We have customers."

Jones closed the door behind him and touched the brim of his hat. "Much obliged, ma'am."

"Certainly, we at the United States Postal Service are always happy to assist our fellow agents."

"Thank you, Postmaster..." Jones hung it out there, waiting for her to fill in the last name.

"Oh, I'm not the Postmaster, he's in Des Moines this week. I'm Officer in Charge in his absence. Name's Deloris Williams, now how can I be of assistance?"

"We need a physical address for a person holding a PO box here."

"Absolutely, what's the name and the box number?"

Jones provided the information and Deloris scurried over to a computer and went to work. Her fingers worked the keys like a pianist at Carnegie Hall, and in no time, she came back with the information.

"Oh, I know this one," she said, handing him the printout. "He's an odd bird. His face looks like something chewed on it," she muttered.

"Well, I thank you for your service, OIC Williams,"

"Likewise," she said, adjusting her bosom. "You stop back anytime you need the assistance of the US Postal Service."

"Will do, ma'am," Jones said, tipping his Stetson.

In moments he and Sabo were out the door and in the car. Jones punched the address into the Volkswagen's GPS and Sabo called Charlotte.

***

They had just started on the trail when Charlotte's phone rang. She answered on the first ring. Stu brought Apex to heel; the huge animal didn't like being stopped and was vocal about it.

"Sabo?" she yelled into the phone, pressing the palm of her hand against her free ear. "Say it again, I can't hear you with this friggin' dog barking."

"He's not a radio, I can't just turn him off," Stu said, then he turned to Sully. "You stay with her, I'll take Apex outside."

Sully gave his friend the thumbs-up and the noise moved quickly away. Charlotte exhaled in frustration. "Sorry, Sabo. Give that to me again." She listened and jotted the information down on her notepad. "Awesome, see you there," she said, and hung up. "Sully, we gotta break away from this. Or at least I have to."

Sully tossed her his keys. "You go ahead," he said and handed her his business card. "That's my cell number. Call me when you have a minute so I have your number and can tell you where to pick me up later."

Charlotte took the card and punched his number into her phone.

Sully's phone rang. He looked at his screen and hit the end call button. "Got it. Okay, well good luck, and please be careful."

The words were genuine and so was the look in his eyes. Sully was a nice guy, and she sure wished she'd had the conversation with Alex that she had been meaning to have. She'd known for some time that their relationship was dead. It had gotten to the point where she didn't care when he didn't come home. She didn't even care *why* he didn't come home. All she knew was that the sound of his key

in the door made her skin crawl, made her wish
her phone would ring and drag her away from the
phony pleasantries and the look he always wore —
the one that he thought made him look like a loving
husband and partner, but that she read as the sappy
mask of a betrayer.

Charlotte pushed the thoughts of her failed mar-
riage out of her head and entered the address in
her phone, not having the first idea how to operate
Sully's in-car GPS. But before she did, she looked
at his number one more time and smiled. She was
definitely taking him out for a drink when she was
clear of Alex and all of his bullshit.

After a few turns, she saw that she had fifteen
miles to go before her next turn and interrupted the
GPS on her phone. She dialed 911 and requested ad-
ditional units and an ambulance to 0S906 Oehlerking Road. Then she found the switch for the overheads and siren and pinned the accelerator to the
floor.

27

Chapter 27

Friday, May 10, 2019
Oehlerking Farm, Rural-Iowa

Rodney pushed harder on the handle and pinned her head in place. The tool banged off Seneca's tooth and triggered the exposed nerve. Her eyes rolled wildly in her head, and she screamed even though her tongue was being pushed back in her throat by the wooden handle. Rodney opened the nail puller and forced it into her mouth.

"Hold still! Mother was only missing two teeth; you keep moving around, and I'm liable to clip off more than that."

The metal prongs bit down on her tooth, and Rodney squeezed the handles together. The tooth snapped off right in line with the first, and he pulled the hatchet handle out of Seneca's mouth.

"There we go," he said and then forced a styptic block into the gap to stop the bleeding.

A shrill gravely wail rose from Seneca's throat.

"When I was a boy, I asked Mother why she was missing her two front teeth. She said they were bad, and a bad tooth can poison the whole system, and we can't have that. Not if the dark thing is going to use you to bring mother back," he said as he dropped Seneca's teeth into a small bag. "We'll get you dressed, and then we can start."

Seneca's eyes were wide with fear. "Use me? Use me how?" she cried through blood-stained lips.

"You're the vessel I'm going to use to bring mother back," he said, removing the blood-covered plastic cape and sliding a white linen gown over her head. "I just hope it works this time.

"You're fucking crazy!"

Raged filled Ronald's one good eye, and Seneca could tell he wanted to slap her, but he didn't. Instead, he pressed the styptic block into the gap between her teeth again. She thrashed her head side to side, but it was no use. He was just too strong, and Seneca cried out in agony.

***

Ray pressed his palms together behind his back and began rubbing them briskly. It took some time, but eventually, the rope that Rodney had used to bind his hands behind his back began to loosen.

It was a trick he'd learned in college during his fraternity's hell week, and now it was paying off. With his hands free, Ray untied his ankles and then gripped his head and squeezed as hard as he could to try and clear the fog that seemed to have settled there. Seneca's first scream stirred him from his daze, but the second touched a primal fear that sent him to his feet, out into the hall, toward the stairs that would lead him to the first floor and out the front door to freedom. But when he reached the stairs, he stopped.

"You don't owe that bitch a thang," said the voice in his head. "Get yo skinny ass down those stairs and out the door!"

Ray's breathing quickened, and he shook his head hard. "Shut the fuck up," Ray said as he turned away from the stairs and moved back across the hall. He stood at the door and could hear Seneca's cries for help. Ray reared back and kicked the door open to find Rodney holding Seneca up in one arm and sliding a noose around her neck with his free hand. Seneca twisted and contorted her powerful little body, but Rodney had no difficulty securing the rope around her neck. Ray crossed the room at a dead sprint and drove his shoulder into Rodney's exposed midsection. Rodney let out a great *oomph as he* flew backward, grabbing a lock of Ray's hair ripping it from the roots. The force of the blow sent

Rodney's body crashing through the window to the ground two stories below.

Ray scrambled to his feet and shielded his eyes from the light that came pouring through the broken window. He grabbed Seneca around the knees and lifted, but the noose had already tightened, and he could see the blood vessels in her face and eyes were beginning to burst. He tried to reach up with one hand, but it was no use. He was much shorter than Rodney and needed something to stand on. He looked frantically around the room and saw the chair. He had to let her go to reach the chair but feared that even one more second would be enough to steal her away forever.

***

Billy Parks could hear the approaching sirens and assumed they were coming for him. He ran off the road into a tree line and hid. He needed a minute to think. Oddly, he thought of his father. He'd never admitted it before, not even to himself, but he hated his father. He remembered how he kicked and screamed and begged *after* the cops had the cuffs on him, how he obeyed when they told him to get down on his knees and put his hands behind his back.

"Fucking coward."

The no-good-piece-of-shit was a coward for letting the cops lock him in a cage like an animal.

He was a coward because when they went to see him, right after he got locked away and was still in the appeal process, his father would shuffle around in shackles and avert his eyes when the big black inmates used to say things about their mother. It made Billy sick to his stomach.

His dad was a big man in their house and talked a big game. He was always bragging about how he was going to kick this guy's ass or that guy's ass, but he never did anything more than talk. Except with Billy's mom. He used to knock the shit out of her. Billy knew she hated him. He also knew the only reason she took him and Joey to see the bastard was because she was afraid he would get out on appeal, and then she would really be in trouble.

Yes, deep down, Billy knew his father was a little bitch. As far as he knew, his father had never even been in a real fight, and here he was, fifteen years old, with more fights under his belt than his father had years in prison and two dead bodies to which he could lay claim. Prison was for bitches, and Billy Parks was no bitch.

***

Ray let her go. In a panicked dash, he grabbed the chair and set her feet on it, but her legs buckled.

"No!" he cried and jumped up on the chair, lifting her body.

Ray wasn't a powerful man, but he found the

strength to hold her up and loosen the rope. She fell into his arms, knocking them both to the ground. Ray rolled Seneca off him and got to his feet. He ran over to the window and peered down. There, splayed out and showered in broken glass, lay the body of the man he thought he'd killed earlier. The oddly molten-looking head cocked at a disturbing angle so that the back of it lay partially pinned behind the right shoulder. Ray could see the bones of his spinal column gleaming with a black viscous fluid in the evening's softening sun. Satisfied that he'd finally killed the bastard, Ray walked back over to Seneca.

"Seneca, come on, baby, we gotta go."

She was slow to respond. For the first few minutes, all she was capable of was coughing and trying to breathe, but she came around and opened her blood-soaked eyes.

"Ray?" she said somewhere between a question and a plea.

"I'm here, Seneca, I'm here," he said. "Do you think you can walk? We gotta get the fuck out of here."

She mumbled incoherently as he helped her to her feet.

Together they made their way out of the room and down the stairs. They took them one at a time, careful not to trip over one another but needing to lean on each other for support. They reached the first floor, and Ray picked up his guitar case.

"I wouldn't leave you behind," he said.

A cool breeze flowed in through the big hole in the front door, and sirens grew louder in the distance. Ray smiled at Seneca, who seemed to do her best to smile back. Ray turned the knob, and, unlike moments earlier, it swung open effortlessly. Together they stepped out onto the porch and stopped dead, surprised by what greeted them.

28

Chapter 28

Friday, May 10, 2019
Tabor County, Iowa

C harlotte could see the rooster tail of dust rise up behind her. Roads like this always made her nervous. You could never tell where the next driveway was hiding, but she didn't dare slow down. She would be hitting Oehlerking Road in less than a mile. All that mattered was saving Seneca.

***

Jones could hear sirens coming from all directions. According to the GPS, his destination was six hundred feet ahead, and he was supposed to make a left. He drove along the hedgerow of dead and broken branches, looking for the turn and then the driveway. He was torn. He knew he should wait for backup, but any minute wasted might be Seneca's last.

"Sabo, you carrying?"

"Fuck yeah."

A gunshot split the wailing of the sirens, and Jones ducked instinctively but hit the gas.

29

Chapter 29

Friday, May 10, 2019
Oehlerking Farm, Rural, Tabor County, Iowa

R ay and Seneca stared at the little boy who stood at the top of the stairs to the porch. The kid stepped a little closer, tilted his head and spoke.

"This your house, mister?"

Ray shook his head violently. "No, and you gotta get the hell out of here, kid!"

With that, Billy Parks raised the revolver and fired one last shot. The bullet tore into Ray's chest, and he dropped his guitar case. The old Gibson L-50 Archtop rang out in a clear, mournful tone as Ray Borowski dropped to his knees. Seneca wanted to scream, but she couldn't. She stood speechless, her eyes wide with fear. But it wasn't the boy who had stolen her voice.

Rodney Oehlerking, his neck cocked grotesquely to one side, the bones poking through his flesh, shambled up onto the porch. With his hatchet in hand, Rodney grabbed Billy Parks by the hair, ripped his head back and dragged the blade across the boy's throat. Billy's blood sprayed hot from the gash.

"Run!" Ray, down on his knees sitting back on his heels, forced the word with his dying breath and collapsed onto his side.

Though Ray's last word was little more than a raspy whisper, it went off in Seneca's head like a starter's pistol. Seneca bolted like a racehorse from the starting gate, clearing the porch steps in a single bound, knocking Rodney to the ground. When she reached the car, she glanced back over her shoulder. She wanted to go back for Ray, but she did as he told her. Seneca reached the end of the driveway and turned right.

***

Rodney disregarded his intruders. Ray was clearly dying, and Seneca most certainly was not the vessel he needed. The boy, on the other hand, could still prove useful. Rodney knelt and scooped Billy Parks up in his arms. He carried Billy to the shed, went in, and kicked aside a rusted old milk crate revealing a metal ring to a trapdoor in the floorboards. Down, down, down into the cold dark earth, Rodney carried the boy's body and laid him on the floor in the old root cellar. "It had to be this way son, I'm so tired, and I need someone to look after the place in case momma comes back," he said and nodded toward a mummified skeleton lying on an earthen altar across the room. Rodney grabbed up a handful of dirt and packed the gash in his neck. Then he whispered, "The old place is yours now. The dark thing will see to your wound." With that, he turned and went back top-side. Rodney stepped out and locked the shed. He looked at his house, everything hanging sideways because of his broken neck, and walked over to the porch, where he sat down next to what used to be Ray Borowski. He stared out toward the road where a white Volkswagen Atlas turned into his driveway and slid to a stop behind his rusty old car.

***

Charlotte pulled up in the unmarked squad and didn't bother killing the engine. She slammed the car in park and jumped out, gun in hand. Jones was closing the distance on Rodney Oehlerking and yelling commands, though she couldn't hear what he was saying over the rise and fall of the siren. She watched as Rodney stood and picked up a hatchet. She could tell Jones was telling him to drop it. He kept making a jutting motion with the gun, and then it went off. The bullet struck Rodney square in the chest and he went down just as she reached National Jones's side.

Several more squads came tearing into the driveway and officers rushed out. The last car that pulled in stayed farther back. The officer got out and opened the back door. Seneca, who flagged down the officer when she spotted him, stepped out of the car and tried to run for Ray, but the officer grabbed her around the waist and held her tightly.

"Please, miss, I can't let you go up there."

"But he saved my life!"

"Yes," the officer said, "now let us save him." As he watched the others on scene holster their weapons, the officer keyed up, "Scene's secure, send the medics up."

The ambulance stopped first to check on Seneca, but she screamed at them to take care of Ray. One of the three medics on board stayed with her as the other two grabbed their bags and ran to the porch. Seneca watched as they dropped their gear and checked Ray. She saw the medic shake his head, signaling that there was nothing they could do for him. To her, it all happened in slow motion. Something broke in her chest, then to her horror, she saw the medic on the ground near Rodney wave the stretcher over.

"No, no, no!" she cried and pulled free of the officer's grip. She ran toward Rodney and saw his hatchet on the ground. It seemed the only thing that was going to kill him was removing his head from his shoulders. She dove for the hatchet, and Charlotte dove on top of her.

"What are you doing?" Seneca screamed. "We have to kill him!"

"I can't let you do that, Ms. Campbell."

Seneca squirmed and struggled and would have hacked away at Charlotte if she had the chance, but Sabo ripped the hatchet out of her hand and handcuffed her with Jones's help.

"Get the fuck off me!" Seneca kicked and lunged at anyone who came near her, but she finally broke down as the medics loaded Rodney Oehlerking's body onto the gurney. "You don't understand," she cried. "You can't save him!"

Sabo took her by the shoulders and turned her away. "Seneca, it's me, Sabo. You're safe now."Charlotte stood at the bottom of the stairs staring down at the Colt Python. Then she squatted down, slid her pen into the barrel, and opened the cylinder using a tissue, careful not to disturb any evidence.

* * *

"It's empty. I think we found Lawson's service weapon."

"The one the boy took?" Jones asked.

"Yeah, and if the gun is here, the boy is probably close by." Charlotte stood up and scanned the area. "I need an evidence tech to secure this weapon," she said, but no one responded. Slowly, she became aware of the bleating of the sirens. "Someone shut those damned things off and then get me an ET!"

One by one, the sirens died, and she repeated herself. "I need this gun secured, and we need to fan out and find Billy Parks. I don't know if this was the only weapon he had," she paused. "But let's remember, he's a little boy, and he's probably scared."

Seneca, who had been inconsolable since one of the officers pulled a blanket from his trunk and laid it over Ray's body, suddenly burst out laughing.

"What's so funny, Ms. Campbell?" Charlotte recognized her from the photos, though she thought she looked much older now.

"He ain't scared," she said, stifling her laughter.

"How do you know that, Ms. Campbell?" Jones asked. "Do you know where he is?"

"He's dead," she said through a sardonic smile. "The little fucker is dead! He shot Ray, and that fucking animal," she jutted her chin toward the ambulance, "did the one good thing he probably ever done in his whole life. He slit that little monster's throat," she said, and looked down at the blood-soaked porch.

Charlotte stepped away from the porch and walked toward the yard. *Could I have missed the body? Did he stumble off somewhere and die?* Charlotte knew all about tunnel vision in high-stress situations, but she was sure she wouldn't have missed the body of a dead little boy.

"You okay?" Jones asked, following behind.

"No, not at all; you?"

Jones shook his head. "To tell you the truth, I feel numb."

"Yeah, I guess I kind of—"

Their conversation was interrupted by one of the paramedics. "Can one of you ride with us?"

"I got it," Jones said and tossed Sabo his keys. "Meet me at the hospital when you guys are done here," he said and climbed in the back of the ambulance.

The medic followed him in and pulled the doors shut as the ambulance started down the driveway. When it turned onto the roadway, it rolled about five feet and stopped.

* * *

Inside the ambulance, Jones and the paramedic sat in stunned silence.

"I've never seen anything like it," the medic said.

"No, man, me neither," Jones agreed.

"Or—" the medic swallowed dryly "—heard anything like it."

As soon as the ambulance left the driveway and turned onto Oehlerking Road, there was a loud, sickening crack as Rodney's bones splintered. The heart monitor that blipped weakly in the driveway, fell to a flatline, and the bones in Rodney's neck poked through his ashen skin.

"Whatever was holding this fucker together... it lost its grip when we left the driveway," the paramedic said.

"I think you may just be right," Jones agreed and hopped out the back of the ambulance. "Well, you don't need me anymore," he said solemnly.

"Hey, Marshal, where are you going? What are we supposed to do with him?"

"I don't know," Jones shrugged. "What do you usually do with a patient that dies in transport?" he said and slammed the doors shut.

Jones stood staring at the now closed ambulance door and rubbed his eyes. It seemed there was a dark haze hanging in the air in the ambulance. The marshal took a deep breath and pushed it out of his head.

30

Chapter 30

Friday, May 10, 2019
Oehlerking Farm, Rural, Tabor County, Iowa

S tu tried to bring Apex onto the scene, but he wouldn't step onto the driveway. The dog followed Billy's scent right to the edge of the driveway, and though he indicated that the boy continued on up the drive, Apex simply would not budge. And when Stu tried to force him, Apex almost took a chunk out of his partner.

Jones, Sabo, and Charlotte made their way in and began a systematic room-by-room search of the house. While Sabo and Charlotte were looking for the boy or clues that might help them find him, Jones focused his attention on anything that could solidly link Oehlerking to the Tooth Fairy murders.

In the kitchen pantry, he found the coffee cans.

The Tooth Fairy always used the same brand, A&P, in the red and gold cans, but he wanted more. While searching the bedroom on the first floor, Jones found what he was looking for, and it took his breath away. He had noticed scuff marks while shining his flashlight under the lumpy, piss-stained bed and pushed the frame aside. Discovering the loose floorboard, Jones squatted down, removed it, and shined his light inside. Beneath the razor wire and broken glass, there sat a box, the kind used to hold large stick matches.

Jones removed the matchbox, slid it open, and fell back on his ass. The little matchbox was full of polished white teeth. He couldn't say how many there were, not without counting them, but he was certain that there were more than the counterparts back in evidence at his field office. *How long had he been out there? How long had he been taking women?* There in the middle of the room, he broke down and wept. *Is it finally be over?*

31

Chapter 31

In Closing

Wednesday, December 15, 2021
Submitted to Strange New World Magazine

Dear Strange New World Readers,
I am writing to you from an undisclosed location, having just left the presumption hearing for Billy Parks. Apologies, a presumption hearing is held to declare a missing person to be deceased. As you may or may not know, I am a relatively new contributor to this fine magazine, having recently severed my relationship with the United States Marshal Service. I tendered my resignation at the conclusion of the Tooth Fairy case. I have found the parameters that I was forced to work within as a law enforcement officer too limiting, requiring

truth to be forced into a box created by what we understand, what we are able to explain. Life doesn't always work that way. There are forces, unseen forces at work that cannot be denied. Some supernatural, perhaps demonic. Others, simply a part of nature, the natural order or disorder of things. Take entropy, for example.

What I have found to be an unshakable truth is this: entropy always wins. That's right, my friends; the universe tends towards disorder. None of us are immune. Entropy sees no race, religion, or social status. It does not care whether you are a good or bad person; disorder will spread. Everyone and everything is subject to entropy. The best we can do as we attempt to fend it off is to keep life interesting. That won't stop entropy, but at least we will be distracted from the process. What I believe the Tooth Fairy case has shown is that sometimes natural and supernatural forces come together and work in tandem. So, while my career in law enforcement may have fallen into chaos, I have found new life studying these forces and in doing so, pursuing less corporeal foes. More on that in upcoming entries.

I wanted to bring you up to speed on the Billy Parks presumption hearing. In a courtroom filled with oohs, aahs, and gasps, Seneca Campbell, who I have referenced repeatedly in previous articles, gave testimony. In her testimony, she insisted that Rodney Oehlerking killed Billy, and I, for one, believe her. Seneca described what Billy was wearing when he shot Ray. That information had never been provided to the press, and I certainly never told her. She even gave a graphic description of how Billy's blood sprayed the porch like a garden hose. It was a bit sensational, but who doesn't love sensationalism? Continuing with the facts: DNA swabs of the blood from the porch and DNA samples taken from Billy's piss-stained underwear found in the hamper that he and his brother Joey shared proved to be an exact match.

Regarding Joey Parks. Joey stood in the courtroom clamped to his mother's side during the preceding. A large picture of Billy Parks sat on an easel at the front of the courtroom, and the younger brother never took his eyes off the picture. To describe the look on Joey's face as fearful would — and while I hate to sound cliché, there is no other way to put it — be the understatement of the year. The boy was white as a porcelain plate, his lips were dry and chapped, and his eyes... I'll never forget the look of terror in that little boy's eyes. It was as if he expected the picture to come to life, and for his brother to reach out and grab him. I don't know if there is a therapist in the world that can save him.

As you may have guessed by the need for the

presumption hearing, Billy Parks's body was never found. Appeals were made through the press, and again, psychics and paranormal investigators flooded the lines with tips. One suggestion that I find particularly interesting was that Billy Parks was swallowed up by the earth, right on that property. The psychic, a man we will call Mr. G., with a fairly solid track record when it comes to assisting the police, said that the body was too deep for anyone to find. And who knows, he may be right because numerous excavations have revealed nothing, though we could never get a search dog or cadaver dog to go onto the property.

As for the property — the house, the old barn out back, the pigpens — all of it was torn down by fall of 2019. The only thing that remained was the shed. It seems the shed and the property it sits on — nothing more than a 20x20 parcel of land — belong to a neighbor, Victor Ostrom. According to documents found in the house and corroborated through county records, Henry Oehlerking, Rodney's father, traded the property to Mr. Ostrom for a brood sow in the spring of 1964. As of this writing, Mr. Ostrom continues to refuse access to the property. It bears noting that, based on exigent circumstances, authorities searched the entire house and every outbuilding on the property, inclusive of the shed, on the day we captured the

Tooth Fairy, or Rodney Oehlerking, whichever you prefer. And while the exigent circumstances search doctrine allowed us to access and search the shed, we were unable to extend that search to include excavation. I have it from higher-ups that S. N. W. Magazine will keep an eye on the obituary section in Tabor County and, in due time, offer to purchase the 20x20 parcel from Mr. Ostrom's next of kin. Perhaps then we will be able to dig deep and see if Mr. G. is worth his salt.

As stated earlier, this case marked the end of my career in law enforcement. Yes, I have joined the ranks of the lunatic fringe. You see, I believe the stories of the people who report seeing mysterious lights floating over the grounds of the Scab, which is what the locals are calling the Oehlerking property. The land there has fallen fallow. Not even the bull thistle that once laid siege to the fields grows there anymore. In the winter, when the fresh white snow falls, the Scab seems to suck all the moisture into the ground, leaving only frozen brown earth.

There is one other thing that bothers me. After the demise of the Tooth Fairy in the back of the ambulance, which I covered in great detail previously; there was one thing that I chose not to mention. I didn't mention it because I didn't know what to say about it. I still don't, if I'm being honest. Suffice it to say that I saw something in the back of the ambulance. At the time I attributed it to being exhausted and perhaps my eyes playing tricks on me. After attending the hearing, reliving some of the incident through witness testimony, mine included, and seeing the fear in the eyes of Joey Parks, I feel the need to unburden myself of this memory. Perhaps putting it here on paper, sharing it, will somehow be cathartic.

When I stepped out of the ambulance at the end of the Oehlerking property, I saw a dark form hanging in the air above Rodney Oehlerking's dead body. It wasn't exhaustion or bad lighting. It was... it was a dark thing, an entity, a spirit, call it what you will, but it was there. What troubles me is that I let them, the paramedics, drive away with it. The medic who sat in the back of the ambulance with me was also in attendance today. It seems everyone who had any contact with this case is seeking whatever closure they can find. The medic seemed okay to me, and we exchanged a few words. I asked him if he remembered seeing anything in the back of the ambulance after Oehlerking... let's just say, broke apart. He said that he didn't see a thing, and neither did anyone at the hospital, inasmuch as no one mentioned anything. I suppose that eases my mind a bit, but I still don't know what to make of what I saw.

The bottom line is this, dear reader: bizarre

things are happening in rural Tabor County, Iowa, and, in this writer's humble opinion, the Billy Parks case is far from closed. Remember, my friends, stranger things exist just off the highways in the deep dark woods than man can ever imagine.

Yours,

National Jones,

Contributor – Strange New World Magazine

About the Author

Paul VanDorn was born and raised in Chicago's Pilsen neighborhood on the city's south side. He spent over 25 years in law enforcement in one of the cities western suburbs. Recently retired, he spends his days writing, playing music, and yelling at the television. Challenging Entropy is Paul's third completed novel. If you have enjoyed Challenging Entropy, Paul asks that you tell your friends; if not, remember what our mothers always told us. If you don't have anything nice to say, shut your pie hole!

You can connect with me on:

- https://coldfrontpublishing.com
- https://twitter.com/ColdFrontPub

Also by Paul VanDorn

HIRAETH

Officer Joe Kott settled into his cruiser prepared for another long midnight shift in rural Red Hook, Illinois. He planned on spending this night as he spent most. Listening to Todd Zeelander's weird radio show, smoking cigarettes, and drinking coffee to try and stay awake. But the driver of a dark blue 1970 Mustang Boss 302 disrupts his plans, and before day breaks, Officer Kott's cruiser is discovered abandoned, and he is left to find his way through a world that even Zeelander wouldn't believe.

DIASTOLE (Book 2 in the Hiraeth series)

Having barely survived his first journey through the brutal and unforgiving world of the Territories, Joe Kott must once again pierce the veil between the two worlds if he hopes to save the people he has come to know and care for. But as perilous as his first trip had been, it might not prove enough to get him through again. Not without the help of a dangerously gifted 12-year-old girl named Tine and a few other good souls he meets along the way. But if he manages to survive, Joe may finally bring balance to his life and peace to the Territories once and for all.

INAKI

The small Midwestern farming town of Chesapeake Station in southern Illinois has a dark secret. For nearly 300 years, a creature known as the Inaki has fed on the blood of the innocent. Those with the power to stop it have chosen not to, placing their power and wealth above all else.

Now it is up to anthropologist Nick Ryan who is visiting Chesapeake Station to study the Native American Nation of the Mooka'am who vanished in the 1700s, to dig deeper and unlock the mystery surrounding the legend of the Inaki. Along the way, Nick must face the demons of his past and come face to face with the monster that drove his father to madness.

www.ingramcontent.com/pod-product-compliance
Lightning Source LLC
Chambersburg PA
CBHW061610190726
48288CB00007B/2261